Reckless Robot

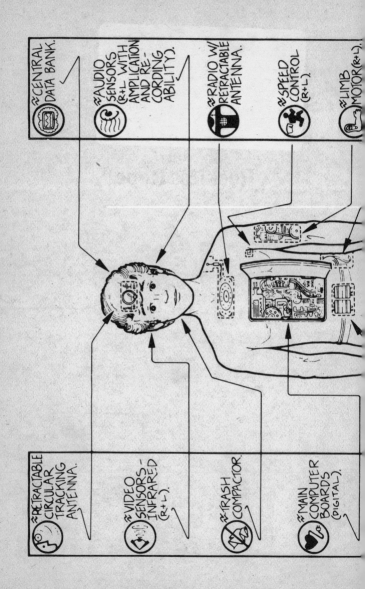

CENTRAL DATA BANK.

AUDIO SENSORS (R+L WITH AMPLICATION AND RE-CORDING ABILITY).

RADIO W/ RETRACTABLE ANTENNA.

SPEED CONTROL (R+L).

LIMB MOTOR (R+L).

RETRACTABLE CIRCULAR TRACKING ANTENNA.

VIDEO SENSORS - INFRARED (R+L).

TRASH COMPACTOR.

MAIN COMPUTER BOARDS (DIGITAL).

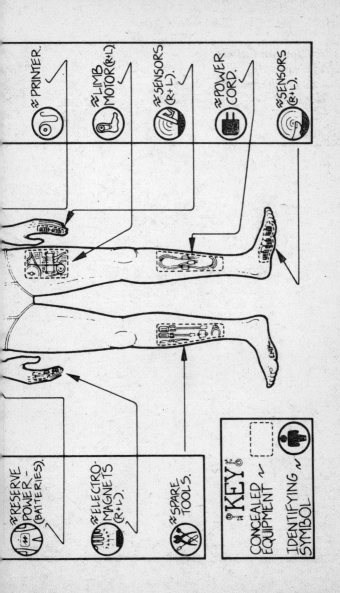

PRINTER.

LIMB MOTOR (R+L).

SENSORS (R+L).

POWER CORD.

SENSORS (R+L).

RESERVE POWER – (BATTERIES).

ELECTRO-MAGNETS (R+L).

SPARE TOOLS.

KEY

CONCEALED EQUIPMENT

IDENTIFYING SYMBOL

In the NOT QUITE HUMAN series

SETH McEVOY

NOT QUITE HUMAN
Reckless Robot

DRAGON
GRAFTON BOOKS
A Division of the Collins Publishing Group

LONDON GLASGOW
TORONTO SYDNEY AUCKLAND

Dragon
Grafton Books
A Division of the Collins Publishing Group
8 Grafton Street, London W1X 3LA

First published in Great Britain by
Dragon Books 1986

First published in USA by Archway Paperbacks,
an imprint of Pocket Books, Simon & Schuster, Inc.,
New York 1986

Copyright © The Philip Lief Group, Inc. 1986
Frontispiece copyright © Ted Enik 1986
Based on characters created by Kevin Osborn

British Library Cataloguing in Publication Data

McEvoy, Seth
    Reckless robot.—(Not quite human; v.4)
    I. Title   II. Series
    813'.54 [J]   PZ7

ISBN 0-583-30985-2

Printed and bound in Great Britain by
Collins, Glasgow

Set in Times

Dedication

This book is dedicated to Laure Smith,
whose insight, help, and encouragement
made all the difference.

Special thanks to: Andrea Brown,
Philip Lief, Kevin Osborn,
Pat MacDonald, and Ron Buehl.

RECKLESS ROBOT

Diary—November 14

If only my wife Emily were alive to see the results of my experiment! She was the one person who had faith in me when I was starting out in robotics at State University. I know she would have been thrilled to see that my C-13 Integrated Electrologic Android acts almost like a normal thirteen-year-old boy. Even Becky, who's twelve, treats him like a real brother.

Chip's high-resolution, multiflex plastic skin looks so lifelike that no one at Harbor Junior High suspects that he is not quite human. In fact, his blue eyes and blond hair are almost too good looking! As a result, we've had a lot of trouble with Erin Jeffries, who has a big crush on him. About two weeks ago I created an emotional response program to help him cope with her, but it didn't work very well. In an attempt to stop her advances, I've installed a new experimental circuit board which uses dynakinetic logic chips to simulate more realistic human emotions. I've also added fifty megabytes of hard disk memory to make sure that he can process all this new information.

Life has been tough on our family recently, but I think things will be a little smoother from now on. When Paul Fairgate, one of Chip's classmates, used a computer to make us look like criminals, it appeared that I might be forced to end my secret experiment. Fortunately, we proved that we were innocent and Paul was guilty. The bank dropped all the charges, and Mr. Gutman, the school principal, personally apologized to Chip (though I don't think the man will ever stop being suspicious of him).

I had better be careful of Mr. Gutman. If he found out that one of his students had synchronized sector motors instead of muscles, he'd throw Chip out of school, although my android is perfectly safe and no threat to the other students. Chip can run seventy miles per hour and lift 500 pounds easily, but he's programmed never to hurt anyone or anything. Even so, I'll be watching him very carefully in the next few weeks to make sure his new dynakinetic emotion circuits don't cause him to go out of control. A reckless robot could be extremely dangerous!

Dr. Jonas Carson

CHAPTER 1

"Look at that!" yelled Jake Blocker. The tall, muscular boy was peering through the window of Foster's Hobby Shop in the Harborland Shopping Center. "That giant model of the space shuttle is great! Wouldn't you give your right arm for one of those?"

"No," Chip answered. "Without my right arm, I couldn't put the kit together. Besides, I think Mr. Foster only accepts money."

"Repairing my dirt bike ate up all my savings," Jake said, running his fingers through his short, spiky hair. "Why don't you get your dad to buy you the model? We could work on it together."

"I'll ask him," replied Chip, "but I don't think he will. He's always saying that I cost too much money. Last week we were looking at a model of a fighter plane and he said that he's spent enough money on me to buy a real one."

"Yeah, my mom's always griping about how much I spend, too," Jake answered. "Look at the tail fins on that one over there!" he added, pointing to a '57 Chevy kit.

The android turned to look. "She doesn't have fins," he said. "She has long red hair."

"Are you crazy? What has long red hair?"

"Erin Jeffries," replied Chip. "I can see her in the window."

"Are you seeing things?"

"No, not things. A person—Erin Jeffries."

"Where?"

"She's behind us and coming this way," Chip explained. "I'm seeing her reflection."

"Oh, no!" grumbled Jake. "Let's get out of here before she spots us. Run!"

Chip had orders to avoid contact with Erin whenever possible, so he immediately activated his synchronized sector motors. The two boys instantly raced out of the shopping center and ran down the block.

"Chip, Chip, wait for me!" shouted Erin. "I've been looking all over for you."

The android shot ahead and zoomed around the corner. He dodged to the right of a troop of Cub Scouts hiking down the street. Jake charged after him but couldn't keep up. He slowed down to catch his breath as Chip turned another corner and disappeared.

"Hey, where did Chip go?" asked Erin as she caught up to Jake. "We had a date."

"That's what you always say, Erin," he shouted as he ran ahead. "Chip didn't say anything about having a date with you," he called over his shoulder.

"He's just too shy," yelled Erin as she raced after Jake. She was small but athletic from years of gymnastics, and she soon caught up with him again. "Chip and I were going to go for a walk today."

"I think Chip is going for a run!" As they approached an intersection, Jake poured on an extra burst of speed, just before the traffic light turned red.

"Look out!" screamed Erin.

A large red truck screeched to a halt. Jake dove out of the way and crashed onto the sidewalk on the other side of the street. When the light changed and the traffic cleared, Jake was gone.

"How did he get away so fast?" Erin exclaimed, as she ran across the street. "Well, who cares about Jake, anyway? I've got to find Chip! If he keeps hanging around with that creep Jake, he's never going to know how much I like him."

"Everybody knows you think Chip is the greatest," said a mysterious voice. "You wrote it in your notebook."

Erin looked around her, but she couldn't see

anyone. "Very funny," she said. "Listen, who-ever you are, my notebook is top secret. I don't like spies!"

"If your notebook is top secret, then why doesn't it spin like a top?" said the mysterious voice. It seemed to be coming from a nearby mailbox.

"You're *not* funny," Erin said angrily. "I'm not going to waste my time on people who play tricks and won't identify themselves." She folded her arms and stomped off.

When she was gone, Jake climbed out from behind a bush, followed by Chip.

"I didn't know you knew how to use ventrilo-quism," Jake said in amazement.

"What's ventriloquism?" Chip asked, brush-ing leaves off his blue jacket. "Is that another name for telling jokes?"

"No," explained Jake. "The name for *your* jokes is *bad*. Ventriloquism is making your voice sound like it's coming from some place else. Can you teach me how to do it?"

"I don't think so," Chip said, after consulting his electrologic index of conflict resolution. "Can you cybernetically vibrate metal objects audio-magnetically to simulate synthetic vocal sound waves?"

"No, I guess I can't," Jake agreed, scratching his head. "I don't even understand what you just said. You sure are smart. Maybe you could help me with my homework. I'm having a terrible time in math. My mom says if I get another bad grade she'll take my dirt bike away."

After examining his data files, the android replied, "You've done a lot to help me. I'll help you any way I can."

"Great!" exclaimed Jake. "How about to-morrow?"

"Why not today?"

"Sometimes I wonder about you, Chip," Jake said with a laugh. "I never heard of anybody wanting to do their homework on Saturday, except maybe nerds. But they don't count."

"You can't do math if you can't count," observed the android.

"Never mind! At least we ditched Erin. You drove her away in a flash!"

"She didn't drive away in a flash," said Chip, "she . . ."

". . . walked away," said Jake, finishing Chip's sentence. "At least things are never dull when you're around, Chip. You've always got something funny to say."

Suddenly the android's auto-focus visual de-tector saw someone with long red hair at the other end of the block. "Erin's coming back this way."

He and Jake quickly turned around and started to run in the opposite direction.

"We'll never get away from her," said Jake, following Chip. "That redhead can run as fast as I can! Let's hide in the movie theater up ahead in the shopping center. There's an old fifties war movie playing at the old movie Playhouse called *Jeep Attack!* I bet she won't follow us in there!"

"Why not?" asked Chip. "Doesn't she have enough money?"

"She's probably got truckloads of money, since her dad's a lawyer and her mom's a bank manager. But I'm hoping that Erin doesn't like old war movies. Most of the girls I know can't stand them."

"My dad says that war is bad," Chip observed.

"Sure, everybody knows that," said Jake. "But movies aren't real, and I like the old ones with lots of action and adventure. Come on, let's go!"

"Okay," replied the android.

When they finally reached the shopping center, Erin was still way down the block. It was nearly time for the next showing of *Jeep Attack!* As they entered the darkened theater, Chip's infrared vision saw that there were only a dozen people inside.

"Not many people are here," observed the android.

"I don't care how many people are here as long as none of them is Erin," said Jake, munching on a big bucket of popcorn. "Be quiet and watch the movie. It's starting now."

Chip had been to a few movies with his father and Becky, so he knew how to react properly. He watched the screen and stored the images in his data files. The story was about a small jeep patrol led by Sergeant Lewis. They were outnumbered as they attacked a huge regiment of enemy tanks.

Just as the jeeps were circling behind the enemy camp, Chip stood up.

"Sit down," hissed a voice behind him. "I can't see."

The android didn't answer. He continued to stand and began to wave his arms. "Go back!" Chip shouted at the movie screen. "You're walking into a trap!"

"SIT DOWN!" yelled another voice behind him.

"Chip, you'd better sit down," whispered Jake. "What are you doing, anyway?"

A chubby girl climbed over a seat and tapped on the android's shoulder. "If you don't sit down, I'm . . . oh, it's you, Chip."

The android spun around and recognized a student from his biology class. "Hi, Stephanie," he said. "How are you?"

"Fine," she answered. "But I'd really like to watch the rest of the movie."

"Why?" asked Chip. "Jake said girls don't like this kind of movie."

"As usual, Jake's wrong," Stephanie replied, laughing. "I practically had to drag

Sid and Mark along. They wanted to buy records."

"Hey, be quiet over there!" whispered a boy sitting in the back of the theater. "Go out to the lobby if you want to talk."

"Yeah, Chip," Jake added. "Sit down. I want to see if Sergeant Lewis will knock out those enemy tanks."

"But I thought I was sitting," said Chip. He examined his short-term memory banks. There was no record of his standing up, but according to his internal gyroscopes that's what he was doing. If he had no record of it, then something was seriously wrong.

Jake tugged at his arm. "Come on, Chip, quit joking around and sit down!"

Stephanie gave Chip a playful shove toward his seat, but he didn't budge.

"Hey, if you guys don't shut up, I'm calling the manager," yelled the angry boy in the back.

Suddenly Chip jumped over the seat in front of him. Staring intently at the screen, he yelled, "I'll help you, Sergeant Lewis!"

"Get back here!" cried Jake.

"What's wrong with him?" Stephanie asked. "I know he likes to joke around, but this could get him in trouble."

Jake leaped over the seat and grabbed Chip by the shoulders. "Chip, don't play around in the theater."

Chip's head swiveled slowly toward Jake.

There was a strange, dull look in the android's eyes. "Are you going to help Sergeant Lewis or not?"

"Chip!" yelled Stephanie. "Quit playing around! We paid our money to watch the *movie,* not you."

The android scrambled over two more seats and bounded onto the narrow stage in front of the movie screen. "I'll help you, Sergeant Lewis!"

Jake raced after him. "Chip, quit it! You're making me nervous! Come on, get down from there now."

Chip didn't respond. His eyes were fixed on the enemy tank. "Come any closer and I'll blast you," he said, raising his arm.

The tank charged in front of Chip. He made a grab for it, smashing his fingers into the plastic movie screen. "No, Chip!" yelled Jake. "You'll rip it to pieces."

Fortunately the screen was made to withstand rough treatment, and Chip's celluloid finger-nails only grazed the surface.

At that moment in the movie, Sergeant Lewis yelled, "Retreat, there are too many of them!" Chip dove off the stage, crashing into Jake.

Spinning backward, Jake hit the first row of seats. Chip crouched down, his eyes staring intently at Sergeant Lewis.

Stephanie raced over to Jake. "Are you okay? I'm sure Chip didn't mean to hurt you."

"I'm fine," Jake replied, raising himself up, "but something's wrong with Chip. I know he's always fooling around, but this time he won't even answer me."

Chip yelled at the screen, "Look out, there's another tank behind you!" Pretending he had a gun, the android began shooting at the enemy soldiers. As each one fell, Chip yelled, "Take that, you slimy dogs!"

By this time, no one in the theater was watching the movie. Their eyes were riveted on Chip. The boy from the back of the theater stormed down the aisle for a closer look. "I should have known it was Chip Carson causing trouble," he said. "I'm calling the manager right now."

"Don't you dare, Carl Decker," threatened Stephanie. "Leave Chip alone."

"Why? Is he sick or something?" Carl answered with a sneer. "If it hadn't been for him and his stupid rock band, our group would have won the Battle of the Bands contest. I wouldn't mind getting him in trouble."

"Forget it," Stephanie snapped. "Just go away before I really get mad."

"Why should I care? I don't let anybody push me around."

Jake jumped up and shoved Carl with all his strength. "Beat it, jerk-face, before I use you to sweep the floor."

"Uh, sure, Jake," Carl answered, edging

back. "If you guys want to make noise, I won't stop you."

Without warning, Chip leaped back up onto the stage. He raced from one side to the other, trying to catch the speeding tanks. "I'll get 'em for you, Sergeant Lewis," he shouted at the movie screen.

"Chip, come down!" cried Stephanie. "It's not funny anymore."

"Yeah," agreed Jake. "Get down here or I'll have to bring you down."

"Don't hurt him," whispered Stephanie. "He's just a little carried away."

"I've got to do *some*thing," Jake replied. "Chip's going to hurt himself if I don't stop him. I've never seen him like this!"

"Let's just get him out of here!" said Stephanie.

Jake nodded his head. Then he reached up and grabbed Chip's ankle as he ran by.

Wham! The 420-pound android fell off the stage and crashed onto the floor.

"Chip, are you all right?" yelled Stephanie.

He didn't answer her. The android continued to stare at the movie.

"He must be hurt!" Stephanie shouted. "Oh, Jake, you shouldn't have done that!"

"He's okay," replied Jake. "Come on, soldier boy, Sergeant Lewis wants you outside immediately."

"He does?" asked the android, his head

slowly turning toward Jake. "Are you one of his jeep drivers?"

"Sure," Jake said. "Come on, outside on the double."

Springing to his feet, Chip raced up the aisle and out into the lobby. Jake ran after him, with Stephanie following closely behind them.

But when they got to the lobby, Chip wasn't there. "Hey," Jake asked the popcorn seller, "you see a blond kid out here?"

"I saw a blond guy run out the front door," she replied. "Is the movie really that bad?"

"No, it's great," said Stephanie.

At that moment, Mark poked his head out of the theater doors. "Hey, Stephanie, are you going to watch the movie or not?"

"Jake, do you think Chip will be okay?" she asked.

"How should I know?" he snapped back. "But I'll never find out if I wait around here. You can do whatever you want."

"I can't desert Mark and Sid, so I guess I'll let you take care of Chip."

"Don't worry, I can handle anything," Jake replied confidently, as he headed for the door. "Tell me how the movie comes out."

"I will!"

Outside the theater, Jake looked all around him, but there was no sign of Chip. "I sure hope he hasn't gone crazy or something," muttered

16

Jake, as he began jogging down the street. "Maybe the strain of the last few weeks has gotten to him. I'd better find him before he hurts himself—*or worse!*"

Suddenly Jake saw a familiar face. It was Erin!

CHAPTER 2

"Have you seen Chip?" asked Jake frantically.

"No," Erin said. "I've been looking all over town for him, ever since you two ran off. He and I *still* have a date, you know."

"Yeah, yeah," answered Jake. "He probably saw you and went off in the opposite direction."

"Thanks for the clue," replied Erin. She turned and started to run back down the street. "If I see him first, he's mine!"

Jake ran after her as fast as he could and soon caught up with her. "You sure are fast," he said, panting. "Look, Erin, Chip's been acting really weird today. I don't know what's wrong with him, so just don't bug him."

"If Chip is acting weird, it's because he's been hanging around with you!" snapped Erin.

"He's better off with me than with you," Jake replied. "Why don't you find some other guy?"

Erin picked up her pace. "Chip's my boy-friend!" she cried. "He likes me."

"I've never heard him say so!"

"Of course not! Chip would only say that when he and I are alone. He's a gentleman, not like you, you Blockh—"

"Don't say it!" cautioned Jake. "I'll sock anybody who calls me Blockhead, even a girl."

"Okay," Erin said. "But I want you to stop coming between me and Chip."

"That's up to him," Jake said with a laugh. "I don't care how popular you are, Erin. If Chip ever liked you, I'd run the other way in a hurry."

"Why don't you do that now?"

"That's a great idea!" replied Jake. "I'm heading for the park."

"Good! I'll go the other way," snapped Erin. "I don't need your help."

Jake smiled as he jogged down the street toward the park. He'd chosen to look there because it was the most logical place for Chip to hide.

"Chip, where are you?" he called, as he entered the park.

There was no answer, so Jake kept searching.

Clink! Something metallic dropped to the ground in front of him.

"Hey, money!" exclaimed Jake. "I've heard of pennies from heaven, but these are nickels, dimes, and quarters!"

He looked up and was hit in the face with a wallet. "Ow!" yelled Jake. He grabbed the wallet, opened it, and saw that it belonged to Chip.

Jake looked up again, searching through the branches of a thick fir tree. He couldn't see anything. "Come on, pal! You don't have to hide from me," he called. "If you're in some kind of trouble, I won't tell anyone."

Still no answer. "Okay, I'll come up and find you." Jake swung himself up into the branches and began climbing. When he was about fifteen feet up, he saw Chip's blue jacket. The android was hanging upside down by one leg.

"I don't think you should do that," said Jake. "You could hurt yourself."

"Were you sent by Sergeant Lewis?" asked Chip. "I'm looking for enemy tanks."

"Carson!" Jake yelled. "That was just a movie. Enough's enough. If you're not coming down, at least talk sense."

"If I come down, a tank might run over me," Chip replied. "My orders are to watch for enemy tanks."

"You sure are acting weird," said Jake. "Look. You lost your wallet and some money. Here." He held out the wallet, but Chip didn't take it even though it was within arm's reach.

"I see three tanks coming," the android announced. "Report to Sergeant Lewis immediately."

Jake sighed and shook his head. "Will do, soldier!" He climbed back down and went straight to a nearby phone booth.

"What if Chip's putting me on?" he thought. "Everybody'll laugh at me if I call his dad and it was all a joke. But he's acting so strange he might be sick or something."

Jake yelled up to Chip, "I'm going to call your dad if you don't come down this minute!"

"Call Sergeant Lewis," answered the android. "Tell him about the three tanks. Hurry, they're coming this way."

Jake kicked the phone booth in frustration. "I've got to do it," he said.

After dialing the Carsons' number, he waited nervously while it rang. "I sure hope somebody's home."

"Hello?" said Chip's sister.

"Hi," Jake began. "This is Jake Blocker. I'm—"

"Jake!" Becky shouted. "Dad, it's Jake!"

Dr. Carson got on the phone. "Jake, do you have any idea where Chip is?"

"Yes," Jake replied, "he's up a tree. And he's acting so crazy I'm afraid he's going to get hurt."

"Jake, there are thousands of trees in Harbor City. *Where is he?*"

"He's in Howard Park, near the north entrance. Do you know what's wrong with him?"

22

"No," replied Dr. Carson. "Chip was supposed to get home by three o'clock, but he never showed up and didn't call to let us know where he was. He's usually good about things like that. We'll be there in five minutes."

Before Jake could say another word, Dr. Carson had hung up the phone.

Jake raced back to the tree and shouted, "Your dad's on the way, Chip. Everything will be all right. Don't panic."

"Why, is something wrong?" replied Chip, still swinging upside down by one leg.

"Hey, you seem okay now," Jake said suspiciously. "Were you joking around before?"

"No, why?"

"Just don't tell anybody I called your dad," insisted Jake. "Everybody will laugh at me."

"Why?"

"Because I thought you had flipped out. You really had me worried for a minute. All that junk about Sergeant Lewis."

"Who's Sergeant Lewis?" Chip asked, examining his data files. "I don't know anyone by that name."

"Now you *are* teasing me!" yelled Jake angrily. "Listen, Chip, you can't play tricks on me like that!"

"I wasn't playing a trick on you," replied the android. "I'm not supposed to trick my friends."

"Okay," thought Jake, "maybe he doesn't remember what he's done. I sure hope his dad gets here soon." Yelling up to Chip, he said, "Listen, Carson, why don't you come down from there? I've got your wallet."

"Why do you have it?"

"You dropped it when you were hanging upside down."

"Why was I doing that?" Chip asked. "What happened to the movie theater?"

Jake laughed nervously. "Can't you remember how you got here?" he asked.

"No," replied Chip. He examined his memory banks and realized that almost half an hour had been erased. Activating his macro-monitoring system, he quickly checked out all his electrologic circuit boards, but everything was working properly.

Everything was—*fzzzap!*

Suddenly the android's body stiffened. "Enemy tanks coming," he cried. "Lots of them!"

"Those aren't tanks, they're cars!" said Jake.

"I'll stop them myself!" shouted Chip. He climbed down the tree and charged into the traffic!

Jake ran after him, but the android was soon out of sight. "How can he run so fast? He's faster than anybody ought to be!"

Chip raced after a black van. "Come back here and fight, you cowardly tank!"

"Chip!" cried Erin, rounding a corner. "What are you doing in the street? You'll be killed!"

"I have to get this tank," answered the android. "Sergeant Lewis wants me to."

"What?" Erin shouted. "Get out of the street!"

Still following the black van at more than thirty miles an hour, Chip was soon out of sight. Erin leaned against a tree and tried to catch her breath.

When she looked up, she saw Dr. Carson's green jeep heading down the street. "Hey!" she shouted, waving her arms.

The jeep screeched to a halt. "Have you seen Chip?" asked Dr. Carson, sounding very worried.

"I just saw him heading down Ridge Road, chasing a black van. Jake said something was wrong with Chip. *Is* something wrong?"

"No," said Dr. Carson, brushing his wavy brown hair off his forehead. He pushed up his thick glasses and added, "He's fine, we're just looking for him. Hop in."

"No, Dad," Becky whispered. She leaned over from the passenger seat and said, "Erin, maybe you could help us more by staying here in case he comes back."

"Sure," replied Erin. "I'll do anything to help Chip."

Becky turned back to her father and said in a low voice, "I didn't want her to come along, just in case something is really wrong with Chip."

Dr. Carson put the jeep in gear and sped along Ridge Road. "Good thinking. We've got to find him soon," he said. "I've been worried sick about Chip ever since he didn't return my call on his internal interface radio. Chip never disobeys. Something must be seriously wrong."

"He'll be okay," answered Becky, tugging nervously at her long brown hair. "Chip's had malfunctions before. It's just like when we get the flu. Right?"

"Not necessarily," replied the scientist. "Why on earth would he chase a van?"

"Maybe he's turned into a robot dog," said Becky. Seeing the frown deepen on her father's face, she added, "I'm sorry, Pops. I shouldn't joke at a time like this."

"It's okay," Dr. Carson answered. "Sometimes humor is the best way to deal with a tough situation. This is one time when I wish this old jeep would go faster. The traffic's speeding up."

"I see the black van!" shouted Becky, pointing excitedly.

"And I see Chip!" the scientist added.

Dr. Carson pulled the jeep alongside the

android. "Chip, what are you doing?" he shouted.

"I'm trying to stop this tank," Chip answered. "Are you one of Sergeant Lewis's jeep drivers?"

"There's something terribly wrong with his logic circuits," said Dr. Carson to Becky. "But if he stops running now, he might be hit by a car."

Thinking quickly, Becky scrambled to the back of the jeep and rolled down the rear window. "Yes, we're on your side," she shouted to her brother. "Jump in and we'll help you." She took a pen out of her pocket and yelled, "Come on, Chip!"

"Good idea," agreed Dr. Carson, steering the jeep closer to the android.

Chip grabbed onto the jeep's tailgate and leaped inside. As he slid into the seat, Becky jammed the pen into his left ear.

Click! The pen triggered Chip's master reset switch and shut down all the android's mechanical and electrical functions.

"That was close," said Dr. Carson with a sigh of relief. "You really came to the rescue, Becky."

"Thanks," she replied. "I hope we don't ever have to do that again."

"So do I," agreed the scientist, as he headed the jeep toward home. "I've never been so worried about Chip before. I'm afraid something may be seriously wrong with him. This may mean the end of my android experiment."

"Don't give up yet," said Becky. "It may be nothing serious. You'll have him fixed in no time, I bet."

"I'm not so sure about that," replied Dr. Carson.

"I am!" said Becky. "You've performed miracles on Chip before, and I know you can do it again."

"Well, if *you're* so sure, then I should probably try a little harder," he said with a smile. "I just hope that I can repair him in time for school on Monday."

"If you can't do it that fast, you can always tell the school he's sick," Becky pointed out. "Maybe I could stay home and take care of him. You could say we had the same disease."

"You're going to go to school unless you've got a fever, young lady," said Dr. Carson, pretending to be angry.

"Okay," Becky agreed cheerfully. As they pulled into the driveway, she said, "I wonder what Erin meant?"

"Meant about what?"

"About Jake saying that something was wrong with Chip."

"Maybe you'd better call Jake and ask him while I examine Chip's circuits," Dr. Carson suggested.

"Me? I'm not calling that jerk!"

"I really need you to, Becky. He may know something that will help me make my repairs." Dr. Carson pulled the jeep into the driveway.

"Okay, Pops. But only for Chip's sake." Becky looked around nervously to see if any of the neighbors were watching. Even though the jeep was parked right next to the side door, she wanted to be sure that no one saw a thing.

"Chip's certainly not getting any lighter," Becky puffed, as she and her father pushed Chip onto a special cart and dragged the 420-pound android into their split-level redwood house.

"And I'm not getting any younger," grumbled Dr. Carson. "Would you please call Jake now? It could mean the difference between keeping Chip as a member of the family and having to abandon the project for good."

Dr. Carson slid the android down the basement stairs on a slide he had installed.

"Okay. I guess I won't be permanently contaminated by talking to him on the phone," said Becky, following her father to the basement phone.

"What's so bad about Jake, anyway?" asked the scientist, as he stood the mechanical boy up against the lab bench. "He seems nice enough. He's helped Chip more than once."

"He's a bully and a creep," Becky answered. "He beats up anyone who calls him a Blockhead."

29

"I might, too," Dr. Carson said with a smile. "If I had a last name like Blocker, I might be a bully myself."

"You, Pops? Never!"

"I remember when I was a boy, a few kids made fun of the name Jonas. When you're being teased, it's hard to avoid fights."

"All boys ever do is fight!" replied Becky with disgust. "That's why I like Brian. He would never do anything like that. Just the other day . . ."

"Becky, please call Jake now! You can talk about Brian some other time . . . and I'm sure you will," he added with a laugh.

Becky headed for the phone, her face turning a bright red.

Dr. Carson opened the hatch in Chip's chest and began testing the android's circuits. The job was easier than it used to be because he'd created a program that automatically checked all the connections between the android and his electronic test equipment.

Information raced across the screen of the main bench computer:

```
ELECTROLOGIC MEMORY BANK
001 , , , OK
ELECTROLOGIC MEMORY BANK
002 , , , OK
ELECTROLOGIC MEMORY BANK
003 , , , OK
```

"Jake's not home, Pops!" Becky shouted with relief, as she hung up the phone. "I left a message with his mom. How's Chip? Is there any hope?"

"I don't know yet. So far everything seems in order."

```
INTERNAL DATA CLOCK . . . OK
IONIC THERMOSTAT . . . OK
DYNAKINETIC CIRCUIT
001 . . . ERROR
DYNAKINETIC CIRCUIT
002 . . . ERROR
```

"There *is* something wrong!" cried Becky, staring intently at the screen. "Aren't the data-kinetic circuits responsible for Chip's logic?"

"That's dynakinetic," replied Dr. Carson, punching several keys on the computer. "They're not only responsible for Chip's logic, they're what make him so expensive."

"Will Chip be all right? Can't you just plug in another circuit board?"

"I could," Dr. Carson answered. "But the same kind of error might blow them right out again. Dynakinetic logic circuits are unstable, and I can't risk blowing out a replacement board."

"What are you going to do?"

"Examine Chip's memory banks and see exactly what happened today. He was fine last night, so whatever caused his malfunction must have happened today."

The scientist hooked up the video recording tapes and turned on the main transfer switch. Digitized images flipped across the video screen.

"Look!" cried Becky. "Chip's in the theater watching a war movie with Jake."

Blip! The picture jumped. One minute the two boys had been inside the theater, the next moment the picture was upside down in the top of a fir tree!

"Hey, how did Chip get there?" asked Becky. "Did you fast-forward it?"

"No," said the scientist. He typed a command and the picture sequence started over again. "There!" he said. "The picture blanked out and skipped ahead."

"Is Chip's memory bad?"

"No, his electrologic boards are all okay. The video picture might still be—"

The phone rang. "Could you answer that, please, Becky?" asked Dr. Carson. "It might be Jake."

Becky picked up the phone, and after a brief conversation hung it up again. "That was Erin," she told her father.

"She must be worried about Chip," said Dr. Carson.

"Naturally. I told her that he's got a fever.

32

I've decided to tell everyone that so they won't think he's nuts. I'm sure they'll believe it. We just had a health seminar at school and the doctors talked about how people with fevers can sometimes do crazy things."

After connecting several wires to Chip's logic boards, Dr. Carson said, "That's a good idea." Dr. Carson clipped on the last wire and flicked a switch. New video images appeared, showing the missing frames between the theater and fir tree.

"Aha!" he cried in triumph. "The images are all there. But why they disappeared is a mystery to me."

Dr. Carson unhooked all the test wires and closed the hatch. He thought for a moment and then reopened the hatch, flicked a switch inside, and shut the hatch again. "Here we go," he said. "Let's hope he works properly now."

"I've got my fingers double-crossed," said Becky.

Dr. Carson pushed a pencil into Chip's left ear.

Click! The android opened his eyes. "Hi, Dad. Hi, Becky," he said. "Why are all the motor circuits below my neck shut down?"

"Just a safety precaution," Dr. Carson replied. "I'm worried about you, Chip. You did some very unusual things today, things that aren't safe. Can you recall what you did?"

The android paused for a moment to probe his repaired data files for the day's events. "I did nothing that endangered anyone else or myself," he said at last.

"Then why were you chasing after that van?" asked Becky. "You could have been hurt."

"My short-range, auto-focus visual detector would have prevented that," replied the android.

"Chip, *why* were you chasing that van?" his father asked.

"My pattern-recognition program informed me that it was a tank—no, wait. It was a van, not a tank. I was supposed to recognize it as a tank, but it wasn't."

"Why were you supposed to think it was a tank?" asked Dr. Carson. "Explain your logic."

Chip activated his electrologic index of conflict resolution. "I can't resolve the conflict, Dad. I behaved as if the van were a tank, even though I now see that its image matches a van's pattern more correctly."

"Chip, run a full check on your own programming," said Dr. Carson. "You can do it faster than I can."

"Okay, Dad." Becky and Dr. Carson were silent as several minutes passed.

"Is he broken?" asked Becky, nervously rubbing her hands together.

"I hope not, but I'm surprised he's taking this long."

Dr. Carson let out a sigh of relief when Chip finally completed his tests.

"I used the new emotional response board to see if I could feel anything about what had happened," explained the android. "Dad, I *feel* as if someone told me what to do in the theater. I followed orders, but I don't have any proof of this."

"Whose orders? Jake's? One of the other kids'?"

"No, I'm programmed not to follow anyone's orders if they aren't logical, and what I did today wasn't logical. I was following orders from *outside*. It was a top priority order and it told me to pretend the movie was real."

"From outside?" Becky cried in disbelief. "How could that be?"

Dr. Carson gasped. "Chip, are you sure?"

"Yes, Dad, I'm sure, because it was classified as a top priority order, and I must always obey those."

"Were you picking up some weird radio transmission through your internal interface radio?" asked Becky.

"No," replied the android. "I don't have any record of the internal interface radio being used."

"But we called you on it several times today and you didn't respond."

"I have no record of your calling me. I'm

35

sorry, Dad, I don't understand. My data files remember everything that happened. Perhaps there's an error in my programming."

"Well, if there is, we're going to find out right now!"

CHAPTER 3

"You kids go upstairs and make dinner," said Dr. Carson, "while I continue to look at these data files."

"But, Pops, Chip said it was something from outside telling him what to do," said Becky. "What if someone else *is* controlling him? They could make him do terrible things!"

"That's not possible," explained the scientist. "Chip is shielded from any outside radio waves except for the specific wavelength that his internal interface radio is tuned to. Besides, who could do such a thing?"

"Russians? Creatures from Mars?" Becky suggested. "I don't know. But how can you be a hundred per cent certain that someone evil, nasty, and wicked isn't controlling him? You're always saying that Chip knows more about himself than you do."

"But that's silly," said Dr. Carson. "Nobody knows Chip's secret, and they'd have to be smarter than I am to figure out a way past all his protective programming. It's just some kind of messy bug, and I'll fix it before dinner."

"Are we having a bug for dinner?" asked Chip.

"No, silly. He said *before* dinner!" Becky exclaimed.

The phone rang. "If it's Erin, I'll slam the phone down so hard her ears will fall off," said Becky, zooming upstairs. "Come on, Chip."

Becky answered the phone in the kitchen. "Hi, Jake," she said. "Sure you can talk to Chip."

She handed the phone to her brother and whispered, "I'm telling the kids you have a fever. You're not supposed to feel well, okay?"

"Yes," Chip replied. He put the receiver to his ear. "Hello?"

"Hi, Chip, how are you?" said Jake.

"I've got a fever," replied the android.

"Wow! That explains it!" Jake exclaimed. "I thought you had flipped out. I'm glad to hear it's only a fever. You really had me scared. I hope you get better soon."

"I feel fine now."

"Really? That's a quick recovery. It must be

some kind of record. Do you think I could visit you tomorrow morning? I still need help with my homework, but I won't come if you're too sick. I don't want to bother you."

"Just a minute," said the android. He put down the phone and went to the basement stairs. "Dad, can Jake come over tomorrow?"

"I guess it's okay, but tell him you can't go outside," replied Dr. Carson. "I want to be positive that you're all right."

Chip ran back to the phone and said, "Dad says it's okay, but I have to stay inside."

"Great!" answered Jake. "See you tomorrow morning. Take it easy."

Chip hung up the receiver and started to help Becky with dinner, but the phone rang again right away.

Becky answered it. "Erin? You just called half an hour ago! Chip hasn't had a miracle cure yet. No, he's not asking to see you. He probably doesn't even remember who you are!"

"Yes I do," said the android, listening to the phone conversation with his audio tracking program.

"Be quiet, Chip," whispered Becky. In a louder tone, she said to Erin, "No, that was just the TV. Chip's asleep, and the doctor doesn't want him disturbed. Goodbye!"

"What doctor?" asked Chip.

"Dr. Carson, of course," replied Becky,

hanging up the phone. When Chip had finished setting the table, Becky taught him how to cook rice. Soon the rest of the dinner was ready.

Dr. Carson came upstairs. "Any calls for me?" he asked. "I heard another ring after Jake called."

"No, just someone selling vacuum cleaners," said Becky.

"Erin doesn't sell vacuum cleaners," replied Chip.

"Maybe not, but she has a vacuum between her ears!"

"Okay, okay," said Dr. Carson. "Let's eat and forget all about her."

"Did you figure out what was wrong with Chip?" Becky asked anxiously. "He's been okay up here, except for spilling half of the rice."

"No," the scientist replied. "I'm completely baffled, but you've convinced me not to give up, so after I've eaten, I'll tackle it again."

"Are you a football player?" asked a voice that seemed to be coming from the stove.

Dr. Carson jumped up out of his chair. "I could have sworn that voice came from the oven!"

"It *did* come from the stove," Becky insisted. "Chip, did you put the radio in the oven before I started cooking?"

"How can you be cooking? Are you a piece of food?" asked the voice.

"The voice is definitely coming from over there," said the scientist. "But the logic is Chip's. Son, were you talking?"

"When?"

"Did you just ask Becky if she was a piece of food?"

"Yes," replied the android. "But the sound came from the stove."

"Another malfunction!" exclaimed Becky. "Now he'll be talking out of the stove." Suddenly she started laughing. "Oh, I can just see it—Chip walking up to school, carrying a stove. I bet Mrs. Crabtree won't ever let him into class."

"Chip, what are you doing?" asked Dr. Carson seriously. "And how are you doing it?"

"I was testing the magnetic sensors in my fingertips yesterday," Chip began, "when I noticed that I could vibrate metal objects. By feeding the output of my verbal response program into the magnetic sensors, I can make any metal object say what I would say. It's the same way that the speaker works in my throat."

Dr. Carson slapped the table in amazement. "Incredible! I spend twelve years of my life building an android, and instead of getting a dummy, I get the ventriloquist!"

"Nice going, Chip!" said Becky. "Now you can play lots of tricks on people."

"No, wait," Dr. Carson cautioned. "Chip, I don't want you to use this new ability of yours

41

again. You might attract attention to yourself and give away your android secret. So you're not to make other objects talk, and that's an order, okay, son?"

"Okay, Dad. I'll—"

The android stopped in midsentence. "You'll what, Chip?" asked his father.

Instead of answering, Chip stood up so quickly that his chair flipped over backward. He spun around and headed for the door.

"Stop!" commanded Dr. Carson.

"Come back!" Becky yelled. She grabbed a spoon and ran after her brother.

"Be careful, Becky!" the scientist warned.

Becky tried to jam the spoon handle into Chip's ear, but the android dodged out of the way and raced into the back yard.

Becky ran toward the door, but all of a sudden she slipped on the rug, losing her balance and falling to the floor.

"Are you okay?" asked Dr. Carson, rushing over to her.

"Yeah, but we've got to catch Chip! He might do something *really* dangerous this time."

"Let's go!" replied Dr. Carson, helping Becky to her feet.

But by the time they had reached the back yard, there was no sign of the android. He had climbed over the six-foot fence surrounding the yard.

"Come on, Dad, we have to bring him back!"

"I know," said Dr. Carson. "If he gets into trouble, I'll never forgive myself."

"We'll find him," Becky said as she headed for the jeep. "He couldn't have gotten very far."

But Chip was already a mile away. He was walking along the top of a chain link fence behind the shopping center, his internal gyroscopes balancing him perfectly.

"Hey, you," said a little boy on the sidewalk, "are you practicing for the circus?"

The android didn't answer. He just kept on walking until he came to the end. Then he hopped to the ground and started running.

Suddenly his path was blocked by a group of kids.

"Chip, where are you going?" said Jenny Driscoll, the girl with curly blond hair.

The android stopped and examined his surroundings. With his pattern recognition program activated, he recognized Jenny, Scott, P.J., and Alex, all kids he knew from school.

"I don't know," he answered. "Where am I?"

"You're on a desert island with a crowd of hungry cannibals," joked Scott.

"Chip, how can you be lost?" asked P.J. "It's not even dark yet."

"I'm not lost," he replied. "I just don't know how I got here."

P.J. whispered into Jenny's ear.

Looking at Chip sympathetically, Jenny said, "Chip, you shouldn't be out if you have a fever."

"What makes you think I have a fever?"

"Erin told me," explained P.J.

"Don't come too close!" cried Alex in mock horror. "You might give it to us. Oooh, I'm burning up already."

"You shouldn't make fun of Chip. He's sick," said Scott.

"Chip, do you want us to take you home?" Jenny asked.

"I don't want to get infected!" said Alex.

"Alex, shut up!" snapped Jenny. "Do you need help getting home, Chip?"

The android examined his data files, but still couldn't find anything to tell him how he had gotten here. Using his telescopic vision, he detected two street signs and calculated his position. "I know where I am now," he said. "I'd better get home before Dad and Becky start worrying."

"Take care of yourself, Chip," said Jenny.

"It's too bad you can't go with us to the movies," said Scott. "We're all going to see *Jeep Attack!* I hear it's great."

"Stephanie just loved it," P.J. said.

"I hear it's a turkey," protested Alex. "I still say we should go to see *High School Madness.*"

Everybody groaned. "Nobody's seeing that bomb," Jenny replied. "Yecch!"

"Not very many people went to see *Jeep Attack!* either," Chip pointed out. "When I saw it, there were only eleven others in the theater."

"Stephanie didn't tell me *that!*" said P.J.

"What else is playing?" Alex asked. "Assuming you still don't want to see *High School Madness.*"

"*Space Pirates from New Jersey!*" yelled Scott. "It's a weird sci-fi movie."

"Oh," answered Jenny sarcastically. "I thought it might be a western."

"Let's go, or we'll miss the first show," P.J. said. "You'd better get home, Chip. You don't want to get worse."

"You're right. I'd better go. Have a good time."

Chip had only walked a few blocks when suddenly he lost control again.

One moment he was his ordinary android self, observing his environment, analyzing data, and following the map toward home.

The next moment, his internal operating system received a mysterious order: TURN LEFT AT THE NEXT STREET.

Chip's electrologic index of conflict resolution tried to stop the order, because he needed to turn right to get to his house.

But the mysterious command was a top priority order. As soon as Chip obeyed and turned left, the order was erased, and a new one given:

45

WALK SEVEN BLOCKS AND TURN RIGHT.

The android continued walking. Data flowed through his sensors, but his internal operating system was instructed not to analyze it or even acknowledge that the data was there.

When he had walked seven blocks and turned right, he received another top priority command: SMASH WINDOW. GRAB ONE MODEL KIT INSIDE. GO HOME.

Chip looked at the store window in front of him. Inside Foster's Hobby Shop he could see the model of the space shuttle, sitting right in front of dozens of other models stacked up in the window display. He raised his arm and *Craaash!* He shattered the thick glass easily. Then Chip reached inside and grabbed the space shuttle box. As he pulled it out, he brushed against the huge stack behind it, causing all the models to crash down and spill out onto the sidewalk.

Leaving the alarm ringing behind him, the android raced home.

CHAPTER 4

"What's that sound?" asked Becky, as Dr. Carson drove toward the Harborland Shopping Center.

"Sounds like a burglar alarm. Let's go see." Dr. Carson guided the jeep into the shopping center parking lot.

"You don't think Chip could have—," Becky began.

"Of course not," said Dr. Carson, cutting her off. "But he might be here if he were attracted by the sound of the alarm."

"It looks like a lot of other people are here, too," observed Becky, as the jeep pulled up in front of Foster's Hobby Shop. "There's Stephanie, Mark, and Sid."

"Hi, Becky!" said Stephanie. "Look what somebody did. The window's completely smashed and the model kits are scattered everywhere!"

"Hello, Officer Simpson," said Dr. Carson, walking up to the black policeman guarding the window. "Do you know who did this?"

Officer Simpson smiled. "Don't worry, Dr. Carson. We don't suspect anyone in your family this time. Probably some crazy kid. There's nobody inside. We're just here to make sure no one is tempted to grab anything from the store before they come to board it up."

"I'm glad we're off the hook this time," the scientist replied. "We've had so much trouble since we moved to Harbor City."

"I think it was just some unfortunate coincidences," said Officer Bailey. "I'm sure now that you're settled, you'll find that Harbor City is the finest city around." she added.

"We do like it here," Dr. Carson agreed.

"How's Chip?" Stephanie asked Becky.

"He's better," she replied, looking around the gathering crowd. "But we may have him tested just to make sure. His fever sure made him do strange things."

"So we noticed," agreed Sid with a laugh. "He was pretty strange this afternoon in the theater."

"Why aren't you at home with him?" Stephanie asked.

"Time to go," said Dr. Carson abruptly. "Come on, Becky, let's get home. Uh . . . I think . . . I think we've got enough groceries to feed Chip for a week."

Becky said a quick goodbye and climbed into the jeep. "Thanks, Dad. Stephanie was a bit too curious about why we weren't home with Chip."

"I wonder if she's got a crush on him too," said Dr. Carson, guiding the vehicle away from the crowd.

"Probably not. She's already got two boyfriends, and I don't think even Stephanie can juggle three."

"You mean both of those boys she was with are her boyfriends?"

"You got it!" replied Becky.

Dr. Carson whistled in amazement.

"Pops, are we really going home? Shouldn't we be looking for Chip?"

"There's a chance he might have gone back there," explained her father. "We've been away for almost an hour."

"What if he's not there?"

"Then we'll search until we find him."

"Oh, Pops, I'm so worried!"

"I am too, Becky. He's had problems before, but never anything like this. Since it looks as if I wasn't able to fix him before, I may have to call off our experiment for a while."

"You can't!" she cried. "You can't just turn off Chip like he was some kind of TV."

"But I can't endanger Harbor City."

49

"He wouldn't do anything to hurt anyone," Becky said. "Even when he was running in traffic, his sensor gizmo-whatevers would have kept him from actually hitting anything. He was just a little confused."

"I *have* programmed him not to cause any damage," Dr. Carson said thoughtfully.

"Then you aren't worried that he might have been the one who smashed the window of Foster's Hobby Shop?"

"Of course not," Dr. Carson replied. "Why would Chip break a window?"

"Maybe because he likes hobby kits."

"He just wouldn't do that," said the scientist. "He'd never violate one of the laws I programmed into his internal data directory."

As the jeep pulled into the driveway, Becky said, "I'll go check Chip's room."

She raced through the house and into the android's room. He was in bed. "Chip! I'm so glad to see you! Where have you been?"

"He can't hear you," said Dr. Carson, entering the room behind her. "Chip's plugged in and recharging."

Becky stood up. "At least he's home." She ran to her father. "I'm really worried about him. What if he just ran away and never came back?"

"He won't," said Dr. Carson, putting his arm around her shoulders. "Tomorrow I'll give his internal operating system a complete overhaul. We'll fix this bug."

"I know you can do it," said Becky. "You're the greatest scientist in the world."

"Not quite," Dr. Carson replied, flicking off the light. "But I'll do my best." Looking at his watch, he added, "I didn't realize it was so late. I may sleep in tomorrow. If you get up before I do, make sure Chip doesn't leave the house."

"Sure, Pops," Becky promised.

The next morning, Becky was up at seven. She raced downstairs and was relieved that Chip was still in bed. The power cord was running from his shin to the wall socket.

She grabbed a quick breakfast, then sat in his desk chair and waited, reading some science fiction books they'd bought just to make it look like a normal kid's room.

At 8:30, Chip's internal data clock told him to stop recharging. He opened his eyes, sat up, and saw his sister. "Hi, Becky, how are you?"

"I'm okay, but how are you doing?"

The android activated his macro-monitoring program. "My circuits are all in proper working order. My fuel cell is one hundred per cent recharged," he replied.

"That's great, but *I'm* starving!" declared Becky. "I should have had more than a dough-nut for breakfast."

After he had stuffed the power cord into his shin and closed the tiny hatch, Chip said, "I could make you breakfast."

"If you made me breakfast, someone might eat me!"

"No, I meant, I will cook food and give it to you."

Becky giggled. "Just teasing. What will you make?"

"I've noticed that humans seem to eat different things each day," observed the android. He activated his random selection program and said, "I could make chocolate pie, pickles, mashed potatoes, and mustard."

"Yum!" said Becky, heading for the kitchen. "I'm glad to see you're back to normal, but I think I'll be better off if I make my own breakfast."

In between bites of granola and yogurt, Becky asked, "Chip, what happened to you last night after dinner?"

"I went into my room and recharged my fuel cell."

"No, after dinner and before recharging."

After scanning his memory circuits, the android said, "My data files are blank on that period, so nothing must have happened."

Becky frowned. "Chip, you've got to stop doing these weird things. If you don't, Dad will have to turn you off permanently."

52

"What weird things?"

"Like what you did last night!"

"What did I do last night?"

Patiently, Becky explained, "You ran out of here after dinner. We looked all over town for you, but when we came back, you were in bed. Where did you go?"

"I don't know," replied the android. "I have no—"

"Yeah," Becky said in frustration. "You don't remember. When Dad wakes up, maybe he can do what he did yesterday and make you remember."

Analyzing the previous day's data file summary, the android explained, "He took out the blocks in my internal operating system."

"That's right," said Dr. Carson, entering the kitchen. "After I eat, I'll do it again and we'll see where you went."

"I'm glad you're up!" Becky exclaimed. "He's back to normal, but he doesn't know what happened to him."

The doorbell rang.

"Who could that be at this time of morning?" muttered Dr. Carson. "Send them away, Becky."

"What am I, your butler?" she asked. "Besides, it's almost nine o'clock."

Jake Blocker was at the door. "Hi, Becky, is Chip better?"

"Wait here a sec. I'll go see," Becky replied, and shut the door.

"Hey!" yelled Jake, as Becky ran to the kitchen.

"It's Jake Blockhead!" announced Becky. "He wants to see Chip."

"I told him I would help him with his homework," explained the android. "He doesn't like that nickname, Becky."

Ignoring him, Becky turned to her father. "You can't let him in before you fix Chip's memory!"

Dr. Carson shook his head. "He seems okay this morning. If Chip doesn't leave the house, then there's nothing wrong with letting Jake come inside for a little while. Besides, I've got a bunch of papers to grade before I start working on Chip."

"Okay," said Becky reluctantly. She raced back to the front door. "Chip is still a little sick today, but you can see him."

"Great!"

"But," she cautioned, "he can't leave the house."

"That's okay," replied Jake, holding up a math book. "Your brother's going to help me with my homework."

The two boys went into Chip's bedroom. In the kitchen, Becky whispered, "How can Chip help that dimbo with his homework?"

"Don't make fun of Jake. Chip can help him because Jake's two years behind Chip in math. Since I've programmed the android in math up to his own grade level, he shouldn't have any trouble."

"Hmmm," mused Becky. "Maybe he could do my math homework sometime."

"But then you'd never learn about the wonders of quadratic equations, integral calculus, and parabolas!" teased her father.

"That's the idea, Pops!" Putting her bowl in the sink, she added, "I guess I'll go learn about some of those wonders right now, so I can have some real fun this afternoon. See you later!"

In Chip's room, Jake asked, "How are you feeling today?"

"I'm okay," replied the android. "I'm all charged up and ready to go."

"I guess that's one way to put it. Think you can help me with my math today?"

"Sure," replied the android. "You've helped me. What is it you want to know?"

"It's these problems here," Jake said, holding open his book. Chip reached for it, but Jake let go an instant too soon.

Crash! "Oops," he muttered, scrambling down to pick up his book. "Just call me butter-fingers."

"Why?" asked Chip. "Is there butter on your fingers?"

Jake's eyes continued to remain fixed on the floor. "No," he answered, "but it looks like your fingers must be a little *sticky.*"

The android touched his fingers together. "My fingers don't seem very sticky," he said.

"Well, then how did this get here?" asked Jake, pulling out the space shuttle kit from under Chip's bed.

"I don't know," Chip replied. "Maybe Becky put it there."

"Yeah, sure, and I'm the president of the United States."

"You aren't old enough to be the president," pointed out Chip.

"Becky didn't put that model under your bed," Jake replied angrily. "Don't try to fool me!"

"I'm not. Maybe my dad put it under there."

Jake shook his head. "No, Chip, it's not Christmas! Admit it, you stole this space shuttle kit."

"But I don't remember doing it."

Jake thought for a moment. "Yeah, that might explain things. Chip, you had a fever yesterday, right?"

"Yes."

"Well, a fever can make you forget things," explained Jake. "A high body temperature does weird things to your brain. We learned that at the health seminar. I don't know why you busted Foster's window and stole this kit, but a fever could have made you forget you did it."

"Stealing is wrong," Chip said. "What should I do?"

"There's only one thing *to* do, Chip. We've got to put this kit back before Mr. Foster finds out it's gone. I went by there on my way over here. They're fixing the window right now. Luckily you knocked over all those other models, so Mr. Foster'll have to wait until the window company's finished working before he can check the inventory to see what's missing. If we hurry, we might be able to sneak in and put the model back."

"How can we do that?"

"I worked for Mr. Foster last summer, and he's so absent-minded that he forgot to ask for the keys back and I think I may still have them." Jake reached into his pocket and pulled out his key chain. He examined each key carefully. "All right," he said. "I've got the keys for the door and the burglar alarm. They should still fit the locks. Hide the kit in something and we'll put it back as soon as the workers leave. Let's go!"

"But I can't," protested Chip. "I'm not supposed to leave the house."

Jake leaned over and touched the android's forehead. "You don't seem to have a fever anymore. I don't care why you took that kit, but we've got to put it back. And we've got to do it now, before anyone finds out."

"But I'm not supposed to go out!"

"You're not supposed to steal either, are you?"

"No," replied Chip.

"And if you return what you stole, it's almost like you never stole it in the first place."

The android consulted his electrologic index of conflict resolution to see what to do about this dilemma and decided that Dr. Carson's order not to steal was much more important than the day's order to stay indoors. "But how can we return the model?" asked Chip. "Becky and my dad aren't going to let me leave the house."

"What they don't know won't hurt them," Jake replied. "We'll go out the window!"

Chip wrapped the large hobby kit in his blue bathrobe. Then he opened one of his windows. "Be quiet," he told Jake.

"Don't worry. We won't make a sound." Jake slipped out the window and stepped onto a garbage can just below.

Clang! Crash! "Ooops," whispered Jake, as the lid fell off. He ducked back inside Chip's room and slammed the window shut.

Becky ran downstairs and knocked on the door. "Are you guys okay? I heard a noise."

"Sure," replied Jake. "I just knocked over a chair."

58

"Don't wreck Chip's room, Jake! He does enough of that by himself! Chip, are you all right?"

"I'm fine, Becky."

"Good. You guys keep it quiet. I'm trying to study."

"We will," promised Jake. Under his breath, he added, "And next time I'll watch where I'm stepping."

Soon the two boys were safely outside and heading toward Foster's Hobby Shop, with the stolen space shuttle kit hidden under Chip's bathrobe.

When they arrived, the repair truck from the window company was still parked in front, but the glass workers were just finishing up their work. Sneaking around to the back, Jake made sure that no one was looking before he switched off the burglar alarm and opened the door.

"I'll go in first to . . . Hey, this stuff wasn't here last summer!"

"What stuff?" asked Chip. "Is it safe to come in?"

"Sure, just don't touch anything. And be quiet," whispered Jake.

Chip entered the rear of the hobby store. His photoelectric eyes scanned the shelves of the back storeroom, and his pattern-recognition program noticed that the room was filled with electronic equipment.

"It looks like Dad's basement," Chip said

59

quietly. He pulled the model out from under his bathrobe. "What should I do with the hobby kit?"

"Give it to me," replied Jake. "I'll sneak up to the front and see if I can slip it back when the workers are finished."

The two boys stood silently as the men packed up their tools and left.

"The coast is clear," Jake declared.

Chip stuffed his robe under his blue jacket while he waited for Jake to return from the front of the shop.

"Whew!" said Jake a few moments later. "That was close. I got the box back to the front of the store, but one of the workers came back to get his hammer and almost saw me."

"Why does Mr. Foster have all this electronic equipment?" Chip asked. "I thought he just sold hobby and craft supplies."

"I did too," Jake answered. "Maybe he's going to have a repair shop or something. I sure don't know what this junk is!"

"What's that in the corner?" the android asked.

"Looks like a dummy," Jake replied. "Come on, let's get out of here."

The mechanical boy went closer. He lifted up a box and examined it. "Mr. Foster doesn't sell clothes. Why would he have a dummy?"

"Hey," Jake exclaimed. "It's a robot!"

"I'm not a robot, I'm a human!" replied

Chip, responding with a preprogrammed response to any direct accusations.

"Not you, tuna-brain!" Jake said. "This dummy is a robot. Look, it says, ACME ROBOT KIT on the side of the box."

"Do you think anyone would think it was real?" Chip asked.

"This?" Jake laughed. "No way, Chip. It's impossible to build a robot that would look human! Say, I wonder how much he's selling it for. It might be fun to have a robot."

"That's what Becky says," replied the android.

"I didn't know she was interested in robots," Jake said. "Come on, Chip, we'd better get out of here before old man Foster comes by to take inventory."

Chip followed Jake out the door. No sooner were they around the block than they ran into Mr. Foster and his son Marvin.

"Hi, Marvin," said Chip. "Hello, Mr. Foster."

Mr. Foster just nodded, looking puzzled as he searched through his pockets.

"What are you two doing over here?" Marvin asked suspiciously. "Were you hoping to grab something out of the broken window?"

"Of course not," replied Jake indignantly.

"Why do you have a ro—," began Chip, but the rest of his sentence was cut off by Mr. Foster.

"Marvin," said the store owner, shaking his head. "Do you know what I did with my keys?"

"You gave them to me, Dad," Marvin sighed. "Remember?"

"Oh, that's right. Come along now. I want you to help me with the inventory."

"Do I have to?" whined Marvin.

"Yes, you have to," said Mr. Foster. "Quit yakking with your friends so we can get to work."

"They're not my friends," snapped Marvin, heading for the hobby shop.

"Oh, grow up, Marvin," said Jake. "You've been jealous ever since Chip and The Deep Six beat you and The Harbor Rats in the Battle of the Bands. Face it, Chip's more talented than you are."

"He is not!"

"Yes, he is. He managed to break up that bogus computer club you were in when he proved that Paul Fairgate was a crook."

"Oh . . . shut up!" Marvin stomped off toward the hobby shop.

"Listen," said Jake to Chip, "why did you start to ask Marvin about the robot?"

"I wanted to know," replied the android.

"Well, don't tell anybody you saw it," Jake ordered. "If you do, they'll know that you were in the store and they'll find out you were the one who broke the window."

"All right," Chip answered.

By this time they were almost back at Chip's house. As they came around the corner, they found Erin waiting for them outside the door.

"Oh, there you are, Chip!" she declared. "I knew Becky was lying."

"Becky wouldn't lie," replied Chip. "Lying is wrong."

"Then how do you explain that she just told me you were in your room and couldn't come out to see me?"

Jake laughed. "Becky was telling you the truth, Erin. We climbed out the window!"

Ignoring him, Erin turned to Chip and lightly touched his arm. "Are you feeling better today?"

"I'm fine, Erin," replied the android.

"Jake, don't you have anything better to do?" said Erin. "Can't you see that Chip and I want to be alone?"

"There must be something wrong with my eyes," Jake answered, rubbing them. "I don't see Chip wanting to be alone with you. Besides, he promised to help me with my homework today."

"Oh, Chip, is that true?" Erin asked with disappointment.

"Yes."

"But I want you to help me with *my* homework."

"Hey, what's going on out there?" said Becky, sticking her head out the door. "Chip, what are you doing outside?"

Thinking quickly, Jake said, "Erin tried to climb in Chip's window, and we had to chase her out."

"Erin, I'm shocked!" snapped Becky. "Chip, get inside this minute! Jake, you'd better go home and let my brother rest. He may still be sick."

"Jake, I'll get you for this," Erin threatened. "You can run, but you can't hide."

"I'm *really* scared, Erin," he replied sarcastically. "Chip, let's work on my homework tomorrow after school."

"Sure," answered the android. "I'll be glad to."

"Why won't you help me with my homework?" Erin asked.

"Because I promised to help Jake first," Chip replied.

"Yeah," taunted Jake. "Take a number, Erin."

"Which number?" Chip asked.

"Chip!" commanded Becky. "Get in here right now or I'm calling Dad."

"What will you call him?" he answered, heading for the front door.

CHAPTER 5

"What are you going to call me?" Dr. Carson asked, coming downstairs.

"Oh, nothing, Pops," explained Becky. "I was just telling Chip to come inside. Erin tried to climb inside his room, and he and Jake had to chase her out!"

"Chip!" said the scientist. "Is that true?"

"No," the android replied. "That's just what Jake said."

"Why didn't you tell me the truth?" Becky yelled. "Now I almost feel sorry for Erin. Jake's a menace!"

"Never mind," Dr. Carson said. "It's time to give Chip a complete overhaul. Something's seriously wrong. Chip, put your jacket in your room and come downstairs."

As the android unbuttoned his jacket, his bathrobe slipped to the floor.

"What's that?" asked Becky.

"My bathrobe."

"Sometimes I think your dressing program isn't perfect yet," she said with a laugh. "Well, I'm going to bake a cake. I hope Chip's okay."

"Have fun," said Chip. After putting his jacket and bathrobe away, he went to the basement. His father was waiting for him, warming up the test equipment.

"Son, has anything unusual happened to you today?" asked the scientist. "Like the things that happened yesterday?"

"No," replied the android. "I've been under the control of my own internal operating system all day."

"But you still don't remember what happened yesterday after dinner and before you began recharging yourself."

"No, Dad."

"All right. First we'll see if there's a faulty connection in your electrologic memory circuits. Open your chest hatch."

When Chip opened it up, the scientist reached inside and turned off the android's fuel cell, cutting off all his energy. Then Dr. Carson began testing each of Chip's miniature memory circuits, looking for a malfunction.

"I can't find anything wrong," he muttered

when he had finished. "I just don't understand it."

Dr. Carson plugged in the android's dyna-kinetic logic boards to the lab bench computer and analyzed the logic patterns that controlled Chip's decision-making processes.

"There's only one small bug," said Dr. Carson, making a note. He typed out several new commands to fix the mistake and fed the data back into Chip's logic boards.

At that moment, Becky came down the stairs carrying a plate.

"I brought you some pecan fudge cake," she said. "So what's going on? Do you really think somebody's instructing Chip to do things?"

"I can't find anything wrong with his programming, but I've fixed it so he'll remember everything that happens to him, even if someone else orders him to forget it!"

"I wish I had a program like that when I have a math test," said Becky. "Don't you want any cake?"

"Of course," Dr. Carson replied. "I'm sorry. I'm really bothered by what's happening. I just can't figure it out."

"Did you see what he did yesterday?" Becky asked. "Maybe that will give you a clue."

"Not yet. I've been too busy analyzing his circuits, and—"

"Too busy even to have a bite of my cake!"

Dr. Carson picked up the piece she'd brought

him. "There's nothing strange in this cake, is there? I don't want to start eating cake and wind up chewing on a clove of garlic."

"That was a mistake, Pops, honest. I still don't know how the garlic ever got into that cake."

"I bet you don't," the scientist teased. "Yum, this is really good. What's in it? I taste pecans, fudge, and something else."

"That's my secret ingredient!" Becky said proudly.

"What is it?"

"If I tell you, then it won't be secret!"

"Fair enough," replied Dr. Carson, after finishing his last bite. He flipped several switches and sat back in his chair. "Now we'll see what Chip was up to last night."

"This is almost as good as watching TV," said Becky, perching on a wooden crate. "But, Pops, don't you want to know what the secret ingredient is? I guess I could tell *you*."

"No, I want to watch this," the scientist replied, fast-forwarding to just after dinner the night before.

The video screen began showing images. "That's Elm Street," Becky pointed out. "Chip's heading toward the Harborland Shopping Center . . . he jumped up on top of a chain link fence. How could he do *that?*"

"Internal gyroscopes," Dr. Carson answered proudly. "He could literally balance on the head of a pin, if a pin were strong enough to hold him."

"Look, there's P.J., Jenny, Scott, and Alex. Alex likes Erin, believe it or not."

"I'm not surprised," replied the scientist. "You'd probably like her too, if you weren't so concerned about Chip."

"Yeah, sure," said Becky. "Don't you want to know the secret ingredient in my cake?"

"No! I just want to figure out what's wrong with Chip."

"I'm sorry, Pops, I was only trying to cheer you up."

"That's all right. I just want to find out where he's been."

"Look! There's the shopping center," said Becky. "Chip's going past Chin's Electronics. See the sign?"

"Yeah," replied Dr. Carson. "That reminds me that I need to go there and pick up some spare parts soon."

Becky smiled. "You must be Mr. Chin's best customer."

"Hey, now Chip's in front of the hobby shop!" observed Dr. Carson, leaning forward. "I don't like the looks of this."

All of a sudden, the screen showed Chip smashing the window, reaching in, and grabbing the largest model kit in sight!

"My own brother, a burglar!" cried Becky in amazement.

Dr. Carson rewound the data tape to the point just before the hobby shop scene. He typed an instruction on the keyboard, and the lower half of the screen was covered with numbers.

"Is this an instant replay?" asked Becky.

"Yes, I want to see what instructions Chip was following when he broke the window. I'll go through it in slow motion. And I had better send Mr. Foster a check to pay for the damages."

"Can you send an anonymous check?" Becky asked.

"I guess cash would be better," replied Dr. Carson. He began studying the complicated codes. Suddenly he shouted, "Hey, that shouldn't be there!"

Becky stared intently at the screen. "What? It looks okay to me."

"Wait a second!" Dr. Carson typed a command. The codes disappeared and the words, SMASH WINDOW, appeared instead. "That didn't come from anywhere inside Chip's system!"

"Then somebody *is* telling Chip what to do!" cried Becky. "But who is it?"

"I don't know," Dr. Carson replied. "All I do know is that the instructions are coming from *outside* his internal operating system. I'm sure of it now."

70

"What about his radio? Is that how they're controlling him?"

The scientist shook his head. "Nope. It wasn't registering any activity at that time. Someone is beaming the commands directly into his master logic unit, probably using a microwave frequency."

"Microwaves!" cried Becky. "I thought they were only used to cook things."

"No, microwaves have other uses," Dr. Carson replied. "But I sure would like to know who's using them."

"We can figure it out!" Becky promised. "I'll help you all I can, Pops."

"Thanks, Becky. I'll need all the help I can get. And I think I'll start with another slice of cake and a glass of milk. What's in this cake, anyway?"

"My mysterious ingredient is . . . catsup!"

"Ugh! I'll pretend I didn't hear that."

Halfway upstairs, Becky stopped, turned around, and came back down. "Pops, if Chip stole that model kit, what did he do with it? If somebody else finds it, they might tell the police."

"We could fast-forward Chip's memory and see," he replied, punching a few keys. After examining the video screen, Dr. Carson replied, "He put the model under his bed."

"I hope Jake didn't see it," said Becky.

"I'm afraid he did."

"But look!" cried Becky. "He and Chip are taking it away. No, they're putting it back. You never would have convinced me that Jake was so honest!"

"I'm not sure I approve of his not returning the keys to Mr. Foster," Dr. Carson replied. "Still, this is one more time when Jake's helped Chip out of a tight situation, and I'm . . . wait!"

"What's that?" cried Becky when Mr. Foster's robot appeared on the screen. "Is Chip looking in a mirror?"

"No," Dr. Carson replied, "but it definitely says ROBOT on that box."

"What's Chip doing with a robot? Aren't they the same as androids?"

"Not quite," said the scientist. "Robots only do what they're told, but androids have the ability to think almost independently."

"But what's Mr. Foster doing with a robot? Are you thinking what I'm thinking?" Becky asked nervously. "Do you know who Mr. Foster's son is? *Marvin* Foster. And he really hates Chip because of the Battle of the Bands thing."

"I admit it's an odd coincidence," said Dr. Carson. "I had no idea Mr. Foster was interested in robots, and a lot of that stuff looks pretty sophisticated. I understand that Marvin has it in for Chip, but why would his father hate

Chip and, even if he did, why would he tell Chip to break his own store window?"

"To make it look like he's innocent?"

"Maybe. Or Foster may have intended for Chip to do something else, and made a mistake. At any rate, Chip was in front of the hobby shop yesterday just before he went to the movie and did all those crazy things!"

"What are we going to do?" asked Becky.

"We're going to get proof, that's what. After school tomorrow, I want you to go to his store, hang around, and see what you can find out."

"Okay," agreed Becky, giving him a playful salute. "Do you think Chip'll be able to go to school tomorrow?"

"I think so. So far, he's only done weird things when there weren't many other people around. It looks as though whoever is controlling Chip doesn't want anyone else to know what he—or she—is doing. But just in case, I'll replace his dynakinetic circuit boards with some new ones I got last week. Maybe that will solve the whole problem once and for all, since the new boards run at a slightly higher frequency. I think it's worth the risk of sending Chip to school."

Becky went upstairs to study. Dr. Carson continued to check over all of the android's circuits, making sure that nothing else was wrong. Finally he finished and sent the android to his room to recharge himself. "I've got to

73

think of a way to trace the signal that's controlling Chip," he thought, as he drew circuit diagrams in his notebook.

Chip got through the next day at school without anymore trouble. After the last bell rang, Erin was waiting for him as he walked out the front doors of Harbor Junior High.

"Hi, Chip," she said. "Can I see you for a minute?"

"Your eyes are open and you're looking in my direction," replied the android. "So I would guess that you can already see me."

"No, silly," she giggled. "I mean, can you spend some time with me? Do you have to rush home right away?"

"You can spend some time with me," he said. "Dad's at a meeting and I don't know where Becky is. I'm supposed to meet Jake at Cap's Arcade, but not for a few minutes."

"At least we can get started," said Erin, taking Chip's arm and leading him down the street. When they were far away from the other kids, she pulled out a notebook. "Listen, Chip, I have to interview someone for my journalism class."

"Who are you going to interview?" he inquired. "Yesterday morning Jake told me that he is the president of the United States."

"That's what I'd expect Jake to say!" Erin

exclaimed. "No, we're supposed to interview our favorite person, and you're mine, of course."

"Thank you," replied Chip, after his verbal response program determined that Erin had complimented him. "But I can't walk with you anymore."

"Why not?" cried Erin.

"My calculations show we're walking in the wrong direction."

"Which way do you want to walk?"

"Toward Cap's Arcade."

"Oh, but that's so noisy, Chip. Why can't we go someplace quiet, like the park? I have to interview you or else I'll get a bad grade. You wouldn't want to be responsible for that, would you?"

"No," answered the android. "You've helped me in the past."

"I sure have!" said Erin proudly. "Without me, you and your dad would have been in real trouble."

"But wasn't it your fault that Paul Fairgate went after us in the first place?"

"Of course not!" replied Erin indignantly. "I can't be responsible if boys go crazy over me."

"I won't go crazy over you," said Chip.

"Oh, Chip, *you* can go crazy over me all you want!"

"Thanks, Erin," replied the android. "But

I'd better be getting over to Cap's or Jake will wonder what happened to me. I'm supposed to meet him soon."

"Well, can I interview you tomorrow night? Or does Jake have that sewn up too?"

"I'm not sure whether Jake knows how to sew," said Chip. "But you can interview me tomorrow night."

"Oh, that would be great, Chip," Erin said happily. "I'll be over after dinner. See you tomorrow!"

"Goodbye," replied Chip, before speeding off to the arcade. When he arrived there, it was packed with kids. By activating his pattern-recognition program, he easily found Jake.

"Hi, Chip, isn't this fantastic?" he asked, intently playing a video game.

"What's fantastic?"

"The video game contest!" he replied. "The winner gets a stereo! Get some tokens and play. We'll work on my homework as soon as I win."

Edging his way through the crowd, Chip went up to the main booth and gave two dollars to Cap, the arcade owner. Cap was an older man with a long gray beard, who wore a blue sea captain's hat and a black eye patch. He was friendly with the kids, and they all liked him.

"Eight tokens," he said. "And an extra one because I like you, Chip Carson."

"Thanks, Cap," the android replied, scooping the tokens into his hand. Struggling through the mob of kids, he finally found a vacant video game machine, called Turtle Rescue.

Since Chip's reflexes were faster than any human's, he was programmed not to play as well as he was capable of playing. A few times in the past, he'd scored so high that kids had flocked around him to watch. Once he almost won one of the contests at Cap's, but Becky had stopped him in time. Today his only goal was to stretch out his nine tokens long enough for Jake to use up his. He began playing.

But suddenly, something strange happened to the android. He received a top priority order: WIN THE GAME. The order hadn't come from his father or his internal programming. It had come from . . . outside!

Ping-pow-zzip! Chip racked up points as fast as he could. Guiding the turtle-catcher swiftly across the screen, he scored so high that the machine began making sounds nobody had ever heard before.

Wing-wing-wing! His score went over three million.

"Hey, look at Chip!" Mario shouted over the noise. "He's got three million points on Turtle Rescue!"

"All right!" cried Cristy, coming over to watch.

Soon a crowd had gathered. "Five million!" they shouted when the android caught a purple turtle in the green zone.

77

Then Chip received new orders from outside: QUIT GAME. RUN OUTSIDE. CLIMB TREE. Without delay, the android let go of the joystick and began pushing his way out of the crowd.

"Hey, that hurt!" Cristy said, after Chip almost knocked her to the ground.

"Where are you going, Chip?" called Cap, coming back into the arcade. "You're the contest winner. Don't you want your stereo?"

Without stopping to reply, the android pushed Cap out of the doorway and sped into the street.

"Cap, are you okay?" Jake asked. "Sometimes Chip doesn't realize how strong he is."

"I'm fine," said the owner of the arcade, rising to his feet, "but some of you kids go after him and make sure he's okay."

Jake raced out the door, followed by several others. Chip was already halfway through the parking lot, running toward a grove of trees at the other end.

"Come back, Chip!" yelled Jake, running past Foster's Hobby Shop. "What are you doing?"

Becky was inside the hobby shop, asking Mr. Foster questions about models. When she heard Jake's voice, she turned just in time to see Chip running through the parking lot.

"Oh, no!" she cried.

"What's wrong?" asked Mr. Foster.

"Nothing," answered Becky. "Thanks for showing me the models, Mr. Foster." She turned and raced out of the shop.

The storekeeper shook his head in disbelief. "Kids!" he muttered as he put away all the kits he'd been showing Becky. "They just want to cause trouble for me."

By the time Becky had caught up to the others, Chip was at the top of the tallest tree. "Come down from there!" she yelled. A small crowd had gathered to see what was going on.

"Becky!" exclaimed Jake. "I tried to stop him, but he wouldn't listen to me. What's wrong with him anyway?"

"He—he has a high fever," replied Becky nervously.

"I don't know," said Jake with a frown. "I think it's more than that." Jake glanced at the crowd that had gathered, then back up at Chip. "This is so weird, Becky," he said. "Chip won a stereo in the video game contest, then he ran outside and went crazy."

"Oh, who cares?" she snapped. "He might break his neck up there! Jake, we've got to get him to come down."

"Maybe I can climb up and convince him," Jake suggested. He grabbed a limb and began climbing slowly up the tree.

When he was halfway up, Chip looked down at him. "Do you want to do your homework now?"

"No!" shouted Jake, almost losing his balance. "I just want you to come down from this tree."

"Why?"

"Because you're sick, and it's dangerous for you to be up here. Besides, don't you want your prize for winning the contest?" he asked.

"What contest?" asked the android.

"Boy, you can't remember anything anymore," Jake answered. "You won a stereo at Cap's Video Arcade by getting an unbelievably high score on Turtle Rescue."

"I don't remember that."

"Trust me. You won," said Jake. "Now, slowly and carefully, come down out of the tree, okay?"

"Sure," replied Chip. "Then we'll go to my house and do your homework."

"Just come down out of the tree."

The crowd watched as the android easily swung from branch to branch, shot past Jake, and landed on the ground below. When they saw that he was unhurt, they began to drift away.

"Oh, Chip," cried Becky, wrapping her arms around him. "I'm so glad you're safe."

"I've climbed trees before," said Chip.

"But this time you've got a fever," she replied.

"Some fever!" observed Mario. "I'm going

80

to jump in the bay, catch a cold, and see if it will make my video game scores as high as his!"

"Come on, Chip, let's get your prize and go home," said Becky.

"I hope Cap won't be mad at Chip," said Jake. "Chip shoved him really hard when he ran out the door."

"You be sure to apologize to him, Chip," said Becky.

The android nodded. When they reached the arcade, Cap was at the door waiting for them. "I'm sorry I pushed you," said Chip.

"That's okay," replied Cap. "I know you kids can get excited sometimes. You won the contest." He ducked inside and returned a moment later with a large box. "Here's your stereo, my boy."

Chip took the huge box. "Thank you, Cap."

"I'm glad you were the winner," he replied, adjusting his blue cap. "The next time you win a contest, don't run away until you've gotten your prize."

"I won't," promised the android.

"Okay, Chip, let's go home," said Becky, tugging at his arm.

"Are you coming, Jake?" asked the android.

"No, you're sick, remember?" Jake answered. "I think you should rest. Or maybe go see a doctor."

"See you tomorrow," said Chip, waving

goodbye with one hand while he carefully balanced the box with the other.

When Becky and Chip got home, Dr. Carson was there to greet them. "What's in the carton, Chip?"

"A stereo," replied the android.

"Oh, no!" the scientist cried. "He didn't steal it, did he, Becky?"

"No," she replied. "He won it in a video game contest at the arcade. But afterward he went crazy again, Pops."

"What about Mr. Foster?" asked Dr. Carson. "Was he around? Were you there when it happened?"

"Your girl detective was on the job," Becky answered. "But all I can prove is that Mr. Foster isn't responsible. I was talking with him when Chip did his crazy stunts today."

"Are you sure, Becky?"

"Positive," she replied, unhappily flopping down on the couch. "Mr. Foster is a little scatterbrained and he's a real bore, but he couldn't have been the one controlling Chip. All that electronic equipment in the back of the store belongs to Mr. Foster's cousin. He was going to move here and open up an electronics store, but they had a fight. Now Mr. Foster is stuck with all that junk. He doesn't even know how to use it. And besides, I saw every move he made. I was in there for over an hour. It has to be someone else."

"Well," said Dr. Carson, "Then we're back to where we started again."

"Not quite," said Becky. "Chip's made a fool of himself in front of a lot more people now! And Jake isn't convinced that a fever is making Chip do all these things."

"I know," said Dr. Carson. "If Chip keeps this up, we'll have to come up with a new excuse."

"I won a stereo," said Chip. "Aren't you glad?"

"Put it in your room, son," replied Dr. Carson tiredly. "Then charge up your fuel cell."

"Okay, Dad." The android carried the box to his room.

"You're not going to disconnect him, are you?" asked Becky.

"I'm afraid I may have to," Dr. Carson said, shaking his head sadly. "Someone might get hurt the next time he goes crazy."

"What should I tell the kids at school?" Becky sighed.

"Just say that the doctors are running some tests on Chip to see what's wrong with him. That's close to the truth, anyway."

"Poor Chip!" said Becky. "He's tried so hard to be almost human. I hate to see it all end now. This is the worst day of my life."

CHAPTER 6

Rrring! Dr. Carson reached for the alarm clock. "It's too early," he mumbled. "It must be the phone." He picked up the extension, but only a dial tone greeted his ear. "It can't be the doorbell at six o'clock in the morning. But I'll check and see." He threw on his bathrobe and slippers. "Who would ring the doorbell this early?" he wondered, as he headed downstairs.

When he opened the door, no one was there. But a small blue envelope was lying on the steps. Dr. Carson picked it up and went back inside.

The note read:

Dr. Carson,
I know that Chip is an android.
Unless you give me $25,000 in 36

hours, I will blow up your house.

The Android Master

P.S. I'm watching every move you make.

"Who was at the door, Pops?" Becky asked, coming down in her nightgown. "It's not even six o'clock yet!"

"I wish I could say it was someone playing a practical joke," said Dr. Carson, handing her the note. "But I don't think it is."

Becky read it. "This is terrible!" she moaned. "Who would do this to us?"

The scientist shook his head. "I don't know. All it says is the Android Master."

"Sounds like a comic book villain."

"But I think it's for real," replied her father. "We already know that somebody has been controlling Chip's actions. At least now we know *why*. But who on earth has the knowledge necessary to do this?"

"And who thinks we have twenty-five thousand dollars to give them?" Becky protested. "Shouldn't we call the police?"

"I wish we didn't have to," said Dr. Carson. "If we do, my experiment will be a failure. Although if we don't, my experiment might be a failure, anyway."

"*You're* not a failure though," said Becky,

throwing her arms around her father. "You're the greatest dad I ever had."

"How many others have you had?" he joked.

"Oh, Pops! Don't worry, anybody who goes by a name as dumb as the Android Master must have a few screws loose. Let's call the police!"

"I'm still not sure I want to end my experiment so quickly," Dr. Carson said. "We've got a day and a half to deliver the money. And besides, this note might give us the clues to find this jerk ourselves."

"We can do it!" she cheered.

"Thanks for your confidence. Let's eat and then we'll figure out a plan."

They went into the kitchen, where Dr. Carson whipped up a batch of waffles.

"Can you think of *any*one who'd be able to control Chip?" Becky asked, as she poured syrup over her waffles. "And can you think of someone who would know about your project in the first place?"

"Those are good questions," her father said. "It has to be someone with a lot of electronic knowledge and equipment. That's why I thought it might have been Mr. Foster."

"But he wouldn't know about your project. Who would want to hurt us?"

"Nobody I can think of," said Dr. Carson. "We're still pretty new in town. At school, only Mr. Gutman and Mr. Duckworth seem to dislike Chip, but they don't have enough knowledge of robotics.''

"Tad Taggart and Paul Fairgate are the types who might pull a stunt like this," Becky pointed out. "But they're still in the Juvenile Center with Nails Johnson."

"Thank goodness for that," answered Dr. Carson, making another waffle. "Well, this note is a definite clue," he said, examining it again. "It was printed on a computer, but I've never seen a printer typeface like this one. Today on my lunch hour, I'm going to hit all the computer stores and see which brand of printer it is."

"What can I do to help?"

"You can wash the dishes and then try to keep a close eye on Chip all day."

"You got it! But Pops, do you think it's a good idea to send him to school? Like you said last night, if we tell everyone he's at the doctor's office getting tests, then he can stay home."

"No," replied the scientist angrily. "I'm not going to give the Android Master the satisfaction! Anyway, it's okay for him to go to school because I've been working on a new device that may help us catch this creep. It will also help me keep tabs on Chip at the same time."

"What is it?" asked Becky.

"It's a new scanner that will track all microwave signals transmitted to Chip. I'll hide it in my desk at school and a buzzer will sound as soon as a microwave signal interferes with Chip."

"Great!" said Becky. Dr. Carson went down to the basement laboratory.

"Good morning, Becky," said Chip, entering the room. "How are you today?"

"Fine," Becky answered. "How are *you* feeling this morning?"

"Everything's working properly," replied the android. "Why are you eating breakfast early?"

"No special reason."

"Where's Dad?"

"He's in the basement working on something. You can help me with the dishes."

"Okay."

"That's what I like about you," giggled Becky. "You're always ready to help."

"I'm designed to perform all human functions," said Chip.

"Let's try out your dish drying. And don't drop any this time. We've gone through one set of plates already!"

Just before it was time to leave for school, Dr. Carson came up from the basement. "Chip, how are your circuits this morning?"

"Everything's functioning at one hundred per cent," the android answered. "I didn't even break a dish."

"Yeah, Pops, if we need extra money, we can

put him to work washing dishes in a restaurant," said Becky as she dried her hands.

"I hope it doesn't come to that," replied Dr. Carson with a weary sigh.

"Why do you say that, Dad?" Chip asked. "Are you having money problems again?"

"Not exactly, son," replied his father. "You'd better get ready for school."

Chip went into his room to get his books. "How'd you do?" whispered Becky.

"Fine," he whispered back. "My microwave scanner is all set up, and I've got it hidden in this cardboard box so I can take it to school. Any problems with Chip?"

"No, he seems fine this morning."

"All right, get ready, then."

Soon they were on their way. They arrived as the first bell was ringing. As the android got out of the jeep, Dr. Carson said, "Chip, if you get any orders from an outside source, try to call me on your internal interface radio."

"I will, Dad."

"Take care of yourself, Chip," said Becky, hugging him tightly.

"Don't worry," he said. "I am programmed to operate with extreme caution."

Chip's first class was social studies with Mrs. Crabtree. When the gray-haired woman asked Chip to tell the class what kind of money was used in Albania, the android called his father on the internal interface radio. "I'M GETTING AN ORDER, DAD."

Luckily Dr. Carson's first class was a laboratory, and everyone was busy on the lab experiments, so he was able to turn his back to his students and answer the beeping portable radio without anyone becoming suspicious. "WHAT IS THE ORDER?" he whispered.

"MRS. CRABTREE WANTS ME TO TELL HER WHAT KIND OF MONEY IS USED IN ALBANIA."

Dr. Carson sighed in relief. "CHIP, ONLY CALL ME IF YOU ARE ORDERED TO DO SOMETHING THAT GOES AGAINST YOUR NORMAL PROGRAMMING."

"OKAY, DAD. GOODBYE."

"Well, Chip Carson, do you know the answer or don't you?" snapped Mrs. Crabtree. "We're waiting."

"The *lek* is the unit of money in Albania," replied the android.

"Very good, but try to answer sooner," she said. "Now, Jason, what is Albania's principal export?"

The rest of the class went smoothly. When it was over, Chip walked out the door and was greeted by Becky. "How's it going, big brother?"

"Fine," the android replied. "What are you doing over here? Your next class is two flights down at the other end of the building."

"I just want to make sure you're okay."

"Thanks, Becky. I'm really all right."

"You make sure you stay that way!" Becky hurried off.

Chip's next class was math. He sat down in his usual seat next to Jenny Driscoll.

"Hey, Chip, glad to see you. I guess you're feeling better today or you wouldn't be in school."

"That's logical," replied the android. "Did you like the movie you saw Saturday?"

"Yeah, it was great. You should come with us next Saturday. We're going to see—"

"Jenny Driscoll!" snapped Ms. Buzzi. "The rest of the class is ready to start. Would you finish your conversation with Chip later?"

"Sorry," said Jenny.

"Now," said the stern teacher, "you may do the first six problems on the board."

Jenny groaned as she rose from her seat. "Wish me luck, Chip."

"Okay, I wish you luck."

At the end of math, Chip hurried to his art class.

When he entered the room, Erin was waiting for him as usual.

"Chip, I've been so worried about you."

"Why?" asked the android. "Everybody seems worried about me, but I feel fine."

"Silly. It's only because everyone likes you so

much that they worry when you do crazy things for no reason."

Erin reached over and touched Chip's forehead. "After all, you don't have a fever anymore."

"No, I don't," agreed the android. "You can take your hand off my head now."

"But I like it there," she said. "Doesn't it feel nice?"

"I don't think you can do your classwork with only one hand," said Chip.

"I could try," Erin said with a giggle.

Handing out sheets of brightly colored construction paper, Mr. Gibson said, "Today we're going to make collages with torn paper. You are not to use scissors!"

"That's kid stuff," grumbled a boy in the back of the room.

"I thought someone might say that," said Mr. Gibson. "So last night I borrowed these record album covers to give you some ideas of what you can do with this technique." He held the covers up for the class to see.

"Hey, the Mutated Mechanics, my favorite!" the boy cried.

"That just goes to show you that using an old-fashioned technique in a new way can create some amazing results. So let's get to work."

"Those album covers look pretty great, but construction paper always reminds me of kindergarten!" Erin said. "Chip, did you like kindergarten?"

"I don't remember," he replied, following a programmed response. "I was too young."

"Oh, well. Let's see if I can tear this paper to make a portrait of you. There are lots of things you don't seem to remember, Chip, but don't forget we have a date tonight."

"I remember," answered the android. "You want to interview your favorite person, which is me."

At the end of art class, Mr. Gibson came by and examined the students' work. "Chip, that's a very skillful picture of a jet plane, but next time you should try to do something more artistic."

"Why aren't jet planes artistic?" asked the android.

"I feel that you should create art from life, from nature!" answered the bearded teacher. "There are many conflicting theories of art, but in my opinion, art is about emotions, and nature is more alive with emotion than anything manufactured."

"Yeah," agreed Erin. "Like this picture I did of Chip. He's one hundred per cent natural!"

Squinting his eyes, Mr. Gibson said, "Yes, it does look like him. You did a nice job, Erin."

The bell rang, and Erin said, "Chip, I won't be at lunch today. I have to meet my mom so we can plan a big surprise party for my dad this weekend. It's a secret, so please don't tell anyone about it."

"I won't," promised the android.

"But I'll see you this afternoon in English."

"And after dinner tonight, too," added Chip, heading for the lunchroom.

"Hey, Chip!" called Alex from the lunch line. "The hash today is made out of last week's garbage."

"That's a good idea," the android replied, putting a plate of hash on his orange tray. "Mrs. Quackenbush says that unless we recycle everything, we'll run out of food soon."

"Quacky's so skinny you'd think she wouldn't worry even if we did run out of food," Alex joked. "Seriously, Chip, how can you eat that hash?"

Putting his tray down on the table where he usually sat, Chip answered, "I just put it in my mouth and chew. Is there some other way?" He was programmed to give this response even though the android had a miniature trash compactor inside that would store the food until it could be disposed of later.

"Hi, Chip," said Jenny. "Wasn't Ms. Buzzi awful this morning?"

Without answering, the android suddenly began piling his dishes in a stack.

"What are you doing?" Jenny asked. "Don't you like the nutritious food that they serve around here?"

Chip grabbed her plate. "Hey, I'm not done!" she cried, pulling it back. He yanked it away from her.

"If you're going to go crazy again, at least let me finish my food first!"

With lightning speed, the android began grabbing plates and cups from everyone's trays.

"Stop it, Chip!" yelled Mario.

"What's wrong with you?" Jenny shouted.

"He must be really sick," said Mario. "I'd stay away from him."

"But he's stacking those things up to the ceiling!" P.J. grabbed her plate of food just in time.

At that moment, Jake Blocker rushed over from the other side of the cafeteria and grabbed Chip. "Stop fooling around, Carson! You'll get in trouble."

The android's synchronized sector motors were stronger than Jake's muscles, so he easily broke away. Chip continued to ignore everyone else as he stacked dozens of plates, dishes, and trays.

"Here," said Christy, handing Chip a plate. "Let's see how high you can go."

"Oh, no! It's going to crash and make a horrible mess," Jenny said frantically.

The tower of dishes grew higher than Chip could reach, so he began throwing plates onto the top.

"Wow!" yelled Scott in amazement. "He should be on the basketball team with aim like that."

"Not on my team," said a deep voice behind Chip. "Carson, if you don't stop right now, I'm taking you to the principal's office."

"You should take him to the nurse," said Jenny. "He's really sick, Mr. Duckworth, honest!"

"Then he should be home instead of messing up the cafeteria!" snapped the gym teacher.

The android continued to throw plates, each one landing precisely on the top of the ever-growing stack. At last, the bell rang.

Everybody stood up and rushed toward the exit. "Come on, Chip, I'll take you to the nurse's office," offered Jake, grabbing Chip's arm.

"I'm taking him to Mr. Gutman," replied Mr. Duckworth, grabbing his other arm.

"Why are you taking me there?" The android spun around and pulled Mr. Duckworth across the cafeteria. A plate was still in his hand.

"You're as strong as a pro wrestler," said the gym teacher. "You can't be sick! Come along or—"

"Look out!" cried Jenny, pointing to the stack of dishes. The huge tower was swaying from side to side.

The gym teacher instantly let go of Chip and grabbed for the giant stack of dishes, steadying it just in time.

Pulling Chip toward the door, Jake said, "Don't let go, Mr. Duckworth, or the whole thing will fall over!"

"I'll get you for this, Chip Carson," threatened the gym teacher, not daring to let go. Everyone was laughing and pointing at him.

"Come on, Chip!" commanded Jake. "You ought to have your head examined."

"How did those plates get like that?" the android asked, following him into the hall. "Why doesn't he let go?"

"He can't," Jake said with a laugh. "We'd better get you to the nurse before someone helps him."

"The nurse?" asked Chip. "I can't go there. I have to go to my next class."

"No way, pal! You're going to the nurse, if I have to drag you."

"But why? I'm not sick."

"You weren't acting very normal in the cafeteria when you stacked up all those plates."

"I don't remember doing it, but I'm all right now."

The second bell rang. Realizing he had only seconds to get to English class, Chip said, "Goodbye, see you later!"

"Hey!" yelled Jake, but it was too late. The

android broke away and sped down the hall before Jake could even make a grab for him. Shaking his head slowly, he said, "I sure hope that lunatic is all right! The way he can run and throw is not quite human!"

When Chip left English class, Erin was right behind him. "Now don't forget our date, Chip. This evening after dinner. I'm going to ask you loads of questions!"

"I won't forget, Erin," replied the android.

"Have you forgotten me?" Mr. Duckworth said, blocking Chip's path. "I told you to go to the principal's office."

"Why?" asked Erin. "He's innocent. I'm sure he didn't mean to do anything wrong, not that he did anything. I just know—"

"Be quiet, Erin, and go to your next class," ordered the gym teacher. "Chip, are you going to come with me peacefully, or do I have to drag you?"

"I don't think you'd like dragging me," the android answered. "I guess I can miss study hall if you want me to."

With Erin trailing behind them, Chip and Mr. Duckworth went to Mr. Gutman's office. "Don't pick on him," pleaded Erin. "He's been sick!"

"He'll be sicker when I get through with him." The gym teacher opened the green metal door to the principal's office. "Now go to your class, Erin, or you'll get in as much trouble as Chip."

"All right," she replied. "But if you're mean to him, my dad will sue you."

"Yeah, sure," grumbled the teacher.

Erin left reluctantly. Mr. Duckworth stuck his head inside the office and discovered that Mr. Gutman wasn't there. "Carson, I want you to wait right here until Mr. Gutman comes back. I've got a class now, so I'll leave a note telling him what you've done."

"Okay, Mr. Duckworth," replied the android.

Chip sat in a leather chair next to Mr. Gutman's door and waited. People came and went, but none of them was the principal. When the three o'clock bell rang, signaling the end of school, he radioed his father for instructions.

"WE'LL BE RIGHT THERE," replied his father.

Moments later, the scientist and Becky walked into the office. Chip told them what had happened and pointed to the note in the principal's box.

"Oh, no," cried Dr. Carson. "This is horrible."

"What does it say?" asked Becky.

"Chip's been at it again. He went crazy at lunch today." Turning to the mechanical boy, he asked, "Son, when you had trouble at lunch,

100

did you try to call me on your internal interface radio?"

"No, Dad."

"That's what I was afraid of. My microwave scanner didn't pick up anything either. This guy has to be using tightbeam ultra-microwaves to control Chip." Dr. Carson shook his head sadly. "I just don't know how I'm going to explain Chip's behavior to Mr. Gutman."

"Turn around, Pops," Becky suggested. Looking around carefully to make sure no one else could see, Becky snatched the note away from him and tore it up.

"Becky, you shouldn't have done that!" said Dr. Carson.

"Done what?" she asked in mock innocence.

"Oh, Becky, you know that was wrong. And it doesn't solve anything either. Chip will just get into more trouble when Mr. Duckworth finds out that his note was destroyed." Dr. Carson shook his head. "Come on, my criminal kids, let's get out of here!"

"Are we going home?" asked Chip.

"No," replied Dr. Carson. "While you were stacking plates and getting into trouble, I did some quick research on my lunch hour."

"Did you find out who's been taking over Chip's circuits?" asked Becky eagerly, as they walked down the hall.

"Maybe," the scientist replied, opening the

school door. "I found out that the letter we got this morning was printed on a brand new dot matrix printer that's very expensive. According to the store clerk, only two have been sold in this area."

"What letter?" asked Chip, following closely behind them.

"I guess we didn't tell you, thinking it might make you worry," explained Becky. "But that's silly, isn't it? Somebody sent us a letter demanding $25,000 or . . ."

"Or what?"

"Or our house will be destroyed," Dr. Carson finished.

"It sounds so awful for you to say that," Becky said, holding back tears. "How could somebody threaten us that way?"

"Don't worry, Becky," said Dr. Carson reassuringly, as they reached the jeep. "The letter may have been the clue we needed."

"So who bought the printers?" she asked, getting into the jeep.

"One belongs to an Edwin Oliver and the other to George Sanders."

"Do you know them? Do you think either one of them would want to hurt you?"

"Not that I know of," he replied, starting up the engine, "I've never met either of them. However, I've got their addresses, and we're going to pay them a visit right now."

"Great!" cried Becky. "We're going to stop them from making you crazy, Chip."

"That would be nice," replied the android. "I'm not programmed to go crazy."

The house at the first address had a FOR SALE sign in front of it. "It looks like nobody's home," observed Becky.

"I see someone gardening on the other side of the house," Chip said, pointing to the left.

"Do you live here?" shouted Dr. Carson to the man who was kneeling beside the house.

"Nope. Nobody does now!" the gardener replied. "The Olivers moved to North Dakota a week ago. Do you want to buy their house?"

"No thanks," Dr. Carson replied, putting the jeep in gear.

"One down and one to go," said Becky. "Where does this other guy live?"

"Fifteen-thirty-seven Wildwood."

"I know where that is," Chip offered.

"That's right," Dr. Carson agreed. "You have a city map in your data files. Where is it?"

"That's the address of Cap's Video Arcade."

"Cap!" yelled Becky. "What would he need a printer for?"

"We'd better check it out," said her father. "Besides, an arcade owner might know a lot about electronics and computers, and Chip did go crazy when he was inside there."

"But Cap's such a nice guy!" protested Becky. "He wouldn't hurt anyone. All the kids like him."

"Maybe he's only pretending," Chip suggested. "Humans aren't always what they seem."

CHAPTER 7

"This is silly, Pops," said Becky, jumping out of the jeep. "Cap couldn't be the one controlling Chip."

"Well, somebody's controlling him, and we've got to track down every possible lead," her father replied.

Chip followed as they went into the arcade.

"Hiya, Chip. Hiya, Becky," said Cap. "How many tokens do you want?"

"We're not here to play games," said Dr. Carson firmly. "I'm Chip's father. Do you have an Epsoki 8023 printer?"

"I had one," answered Cap, tilting his seaman's cap back a little. "But I sold it at a ham radio flea market two weeks ago. Why do you want to know?"

"I've got one myself, but my manual is missing a few pages," explained the scientist.

"Well, that's too bad," Cap replied. "I couldn't get my Epsoki working. It had too many problems. I hope you have better luck with yours."

"Do you know the person who bought your printer?" asked Becky.

"Nope," replied Cap. "Never seen him before, and he paid me in cash. Now, are you kids sure you don't want any tokens? If you buy twenty-five, I throw in an extra five."

"None today," Dr. Carson answered. "This visit was strictly business. Thanks for your time."

"Don't mention it," replied Cap, stroking his beard. "Sorry I couldn't be of more help."

Inside the jeep, Becky said, "That's a dead end. Cap doesn't have the printer and doesn't know who bought it, and the other guy moved away."

Dr. Carson thought for a moment. "I know a ham radio operator here in town who might be able to help me find the new owner. I'll call him when we get home. What's for dinner tonight?"

"How should I know?" replied Becky. "I'm not really up to helping you with dinner, Pops. This is too depressing."

"You shouldn't be depressed," Chip said. "Maybe fleas bought the printer at the flea market. They'd be easy to crush."

Becky laughed. "Chip, your nonsense could cheer anybody up!"

"Maybe you're right about dinner," said Dr. Carson. "Want to eat at the Burger Bear?"

"Great idea!" cried Becky.

"I thought you might like that, especially since Brian works there at night!"

"Brian who?" asked Becky, checking herself in the rearview mirror.

"Brian Skelly," said Chip. "Don't you remember him? He played guitar in The Deep Six with us."

"Oh, I sort of vaguely remember him," Becky answered sarcastically, as she straightened her scarf. "But I don't want either of you to say anything embarrassing to him. He's just a friend."

"Why, of course," said Dr. Carson, holding back a laugh as he guided the jeep into a parking space in front of the restaurant. "We never thought otherwise."

The Carsons walked under the front paws of the giant concrete bear and quickly found an empty booth.

"I'm going to make some phone calls," Dr. Carson said. "You kids order for me."

"Okay, Pops," Becky replied.

"Hi, Becky!" said Brian Skelly as he came up to their booth. He was dressed in a brown uniform with bear claws on the sleeve. "Want me to take your order?"

"No, but I'm free next Saturday."

"How much do you cost the rest of the week?" Chip asked.

Becky playfully punched him in the arm. "I guess we *do* want to give you our order."

"I see your brother hasn't lost his sense of humor," said Brian. "What'll it be?"

"I'd like three bearburgers, three french fries, two root bears, and a cola."

"What will you have, Chip?" asked Brian with a smile.

"The same," replied the android. "I usually eat what Becky eats."

"Chip!" laughed Becky. "That order was for all three of us. I can't eat three bearburgers, three fries, two root bears and a cola!"

"I could," replied her brother. "My food capacity is quite large."

"That's my brother, the human trash compactor. So, Brian, what about Saturday night?"

"I'm working then."

"Oh, that's too bad. I mean, I guess you need the money and all, but . . ."

"How about Sunday afternoon?" Brian suggested. "I get out of here at three."

"I'll have to consult my busy appointment book, but I might be able to squeeze you in," said Becky with a giggle.

"I don't think there's room," Chip observed, looking at the tiny booth.

"How do you know?" she asked. "Have you been peeking in my appointment book?"

"I didn't know you had one," the android answered. "I thought Brian was going to squeeze in the booth and sit with us."

"Sorry, Chip, I'm on duty. So I can't join you," said Brian. "But I'll bring your order right away."

Arriving a moment later, Dr. Carson said, "I called my ham radio friend, and he gave me all the information about flea markets. No, Chip, they don't buy or sell fleas, and the buyers and sellers aren't fleas either!"

"So, what did you find out?" Becky asked eagerly.

"Not much, I'm afraid. The guy who might know about it isn't home."

"What's a ham radio?" said Chip. "Is that something to eat?"

"No, tinhead," Becky answered, laughing. "I don't know why they're called hams, but they're people who like to talk on the radio to each other."

Brian arrived then with the Carsons' order. "Hi, Dr. Carson!" he said.

"Hi, Brian. I'm glad you're over the mumps."

"Me, too! I got awful tired of ice cream. Listen, I've got to get back to work. See you next Sunday, Becky."

"Got a date, Becky?" asked Dr. Carson, after Brian had left.

"Next Sunday afternoon. Is that okay?"

"Fine with me, as long as you have your homework done," replied her father. He looked at the drinks on the tray. "Which one's the cola?"

"I can't tell," answered Becky. "They all look alike."

"The cola's the one on the left," said Chip. "It's bubbling faster than the others."

"Chip, you're mighty useful to have around," Dr. Carson said with a laugh. "You have abilities I haven't even dreamed of."

"Thanks, Dad, I'm designed to make you happy."

"Don't let anyone hear you say that."

"I won't." Turning to Becky, he asked, "Is a ham radio like my internal interface radio?"

"I'll answer," said Dr. Carson. "I was a ham when I was a boy."

"Some people might say you're still a ham," giggled Becky.

"No, not that kind of ham," he replied. "And it has nothing to do with food. Ham is short for amateur. That means a noncommercial radio operator. I used to talk to people in other countries on my shortwave radio."

"How can radio waves be short?" Chip asked. "Isn't a short circuit bad?"

110

Dr. Carson laughed. "Chip, never mind. Let's get out of here before Becky orders something else just so she can see Brian again."

"Oh, Pops," protested Becky. "Brian and I are just friends. You're making too big a deal out of it."

"Then why is your face turning red?" asked Chip. Becky ran out and jumped into the jeep.

"You aren't mad, are you, Becky?" Dr. Carson asked a few moments later, getting into the driver's seat. "I was just teasing."

"Who, me?" said Becky. "I just want to get home and do my homework."

"I can't imagine your wanting to do homework." Dr. Carson felt her forehead. "Do *you* have a fever?"

"Oh, Pops." Becky glanced at her brother sitting in the back seat. "Don't remind me about poor Chip."

"Why do you want to forget me?" the android asked.

"That isn't what I meant," apologized Becky. "I'm just so upset about the fact that there's some deranged creep out there blackmailing us and threatening to destroy our home."

"If you can find out who it is, you can stop him," suggested Chip.

"That's easier said than done," replied Dr. Carson. "It could be anyone in Harbor City."

"It can't be just anybody," said Becky. "It

111

has to be somebody who knows a lot about electronics and has the proper equipment. That narrows it down quite a bit."

"Down to zero," replied the scientist, guiding the jeep into the driveway. "I can't think of anybody who has the technical equipment and the ability."

"Mr. Foster has some equipment," Chip said, getting out of the jeep.

"But he doesn't know how to use it," Becky pointed out. "By the way, Mr. Foster mentioned that he might sell that robot cheap. Want to buy it for Chip as a pet?"

Dr. Carson laughed. "Hey, that's a good idea. Would you like a pet robot, Chip?"

The android didn't answer. Instead, he pushed past his father and raced into the house.

"Oh, no!" screamed Becky. "It's happening again!"

Seconds later, Chip appeared at the front door. While he was inside, he had hidden a pack of matches in his pocket. He ran out the door as Becky yelled, "We've got to stop him!"

"Don't try," commanded Dr. Carson. "Just follow him!"

"Why me?" asked Becky, diving out of the way as Chip raced down the sidewalk. "What are you going to do?"

"I've been working on a new way to stop him," her father called after her. "I'll run to the basement and get it started. Here, jam this pencil in his ear switch if you can get close enough to him."

"I'll try, Pops!" Becky ran after her brother. "Wait for me, Chip!"

The android didn't look back. He raced down the street, turned left at the corner, and sped toward the waterfront.

"I'm never going to catch up with him," Becky thought. "I'd better take a short cut."

She cut through a vacant lot, sped down Taylor Street, and came out on Bayview Drive. When she looked to the right, she could see Chip coming toward her.

"Stop, Chip!" she commanded.

The android showed no sign of recognition as he shot past her. Becky jumped up and grabbed Chip around the neck. But Chip ran on, not even trying to shake her off.

Becky reached up and jammed the pencil into his right ear.

Eeeeeeeeeee! "Not the right ear, the *left* ear," she reminded herself. But as she struggled to reach over to his other ear, Becky lost her balance and tumbled to the ground.

"Ow!" she yelled, as she hit the pavement and scraped her knee. "That hurt!"

Becky scrambled to her feet and sped after her mechanical brother as he turned right and darted across the street toward the waterfront. While she waited for the traffic to clear, she realized that he had run into an area surrounded by a high fence. A sign on the fence read, "THIS AREA CONDEMNED."

"Chip, come back here!" she yelled, hoping that by some miracle he had returned to normal.

Becky ran through the gate and saw the android standing next to an old shed by the water. Newspapers were piled up next to the shed, but there was no sign of people.

Chip opened the matchbook.

"No, Chip, stop!" Becky screamed.

Chip lit a match and threw it onto the stack of old newspapers. The dry, crumbling paper burst into flames and a raging fire raced up the side of the shed.

"Stop, Chip!" screamed Becky, running toward the abandoned building.

The android threw another match inside the shed.

Suddenly Erin jumped out from behind some trash barrels and cried, "Chip, why are you doing all these crazy things?"

"Doing what things?" asked the android, dropping the matchbook.

"Chip, get away from that fire!" Becky commanded. She grabbed a fire extinguisher from the side of a nearby maintenance building.

"Are you okay?" yelled Erin, rushing up to Chip.

"I'm all right," he replied, walking calmly away from the burning shed.

"Good. Wait here." Erin ran over to the maintenance building, found another fire extinguisher, and rushed over to help Becky.

"How did *you* get here?" said Becky with surprise. She was working swiftly to put out the flaming pile of newspapers, so Erin ran to the door of the shed and started attacking the fire inside.

"You can't be the one responsible!" Becky shouted.

"Responsible for what? I had a date with Chip," said Erin, spraying the fire on the floor of the shed. "Just as I was walking up to your house, I saw you and Chip run away, so I followed you here."

Finally extinguishing the last ember of the burning shed, Becky muttered, "Chip's not going to be able to get out of this one!"

Erin ran over to her. "Don't worry about the fire inside. I took care of it."

"Thanks, Erin. I don't know—"

"Hey, you kids," yelled a man in a yellow construction helmet. "What are you doing?"

"Nothing. We were just walking by when we saw the fire," Becky said. "We put it out, though. It barely damaged the building."

"I'm just glad you kids weren't inside," said the man. "That old shed was supposed to be demolished last week. Now you had better get out of here. This is private property."

"Sure," said Becky, taking Chip's hand. "We'll go home right away."

"Can I come too?" Erin asked. "I'm supposed to interview Chip for my journalism class."

"ERIN!" yelled Becky, spinning around and glaring at her. "Are you nuts? You know Chip's been acting crazy. He should be home in bed."

"You're right," said Erin, dropping her head. "It's so confusing. One minute he's doing something weird and the next minute he's fine. I guess I just forgot how sick he was."

"I feel fine now," said the android. "I don't want you to worry, Erin. I'll be all right. Becky can take care of me."

"Okay, but I've been so worried about you," said Erin. "What's wrong with you? Why have you been acting this way?"

"I don't know."

"He'll be okay, Erin. My dad says he's made an appointment with the doctor to run some tests on Chip. We'll find out what's wrong."

"I sure hope so. Can I interview you tomorrow night, Chip?" asked Erin, still trailing behind them.

"I'm supposed to help Jake with his homework then."

Sighing, Erin said, "What am *I* supposed to do?"

"Take up a new hobby," declared Becky.

116

"You know, golf, reading, Alex, anything but Chip!"

"I won't give up on him, Becky," she protested. "He'll be well soon, and then I can see him a lot."

"Good night, Erin!" said Becky firmly.

Erin spun around sharply and marched away from them.

"I think you hurt her feelings," said Chip. "She just wants to be my friend."

"Yeah, sure," grumbled Becky. "Listen, Chip, do you know what you just did? It was *very* dangerous. You set that shed on fire. Someone could have been hurt. Until we find out who's making you do these terrible things, you have to stay away from everybody, do you understand? What if Erin had been inside that shed when you set the fire?"

"She'd have been burned," replied the android.

"So that's why you should tell her to go away."

"But she isn't inside the shed! We saw her going home."

Becky sighed. "Never mind! From now on, you're going to stick with me everywhere."

"All right," said the android, storing the order in his data files. As they walked up the front steps, Chip noticed a blue envelope under the mat. "What's that?" he asked. "The mail's come already."

Becky snatched it up and tore it open. It read:

You have only 24 hours to make up your mind. If you go to the police, I will destroy your house. I know everything you're doing!

The Android Master

"What does it say?" Chip asked.

"It's another letter from that creep who's controlling you," she said, pushing the door open. "This jerk thinks we can't tell time and is reminding us that there are only twenty-four hours left before we have to give away all our money."

Dr. Carson rushed up from the basement. "Becky! Chip! Are you two all right?"

"We're okay," said Becky, handing him the letter. "But the Android Master left another note, and Chip tried to burn down a building."

"Chip did WHAT?!" said Dr. Carson, frantically grabbing the note from Becky.

"Don't worry, Dad," she replied. "I got the fire under control before it did any damage. I'll explain what happened later."

"Okay, Becky, as long as everything turned out all right." Dr. Carson read the note quickly, then looked up and said, "Think carefully, Becky, was that note there when we came back from the Burger Bear?"

"I don't remember," she said. "I don't think so, but it could have been."

Turning toward the android, Dr. Carson asked, "Chip, do you remember whether the note was there?"

"Yes, I remember. It wasn't there, Dad. Just before I got the order to run away, I scanned the front steps. An internal replay of that scan shows me that the envelope wasn't there at that time."

"That explains it!" shouted the scientist excitedly.

"Explains what, Pops?" said Becky wearily. "That this deranged creepo likes to leave nasty notes? Besides, doesn't the jerk know we don't have any money?"

"But we do now," Dr. Carson replied. "I didn't tell you. My grant money came through, as well as a bonus grant for some research I did years ago. We've got quite a bit of money right now."

"I don't know whether that's bad or good," said Becky. "How can we find this guy?"

"That's what I was so excited about," explained Dr. Carson. "While you were gone, I tuned the microwave scanner to track tight-beam broadcasts. The signal kept fading, and I thought my equipment was bad, or that I wasn't on the right frequency. But finally I realized that the signal was moving."

"I get it," Becky replied. "This guy must have his equipment in a car or truck."

"Exactly!" said Dr. Carson. "And since he's using a tight-beam broadcaster, he can't be too far away when he's controlling Chip."

The android spoke up. "I was chasing that black van on Saturday. Do you think it might belong to the Android Master?"

"This might be just the break we're looking for," cried Dr. Carson excitedly.

"Chip's picture files might have the license plate number," suggested Becky. "He must have been looking at it during the time he was running behind the van." She turned to her mechanical brother and asked, "Well, Chip, what's the number?"

"My data files don't go back that far. The information is stored on Dad's nine-track data tapes."

"To the basement!" said Dr. Carson. "We'll solve this mystery yet."

CHAPTER 8

Dr. Carson fast-forwarded the data tapes, searching for the image of the black van that Chip had chased on Saturday.

"There it is!" exclaimed Becky. "That's the van."

"But something's wrong with the license plate," the scientist observed. "I can't read the letters."

"Mud is covering up the license plate," Chip explained. "The bumper has mud smeared on it too."

"That's a good trick," Dr. Carson said bitterly. "Whoever's doing this sure is smart. I'm almost ready to risk calling the police."

"No, Pops, don't!" Becky pleaded. "Remember what the note said. We might get hurt. And it would mean the end of all your work. We've still got until tomorrow night to think of a way out of this mess."

"You're right. We've got to get some sleep now or we won't be able to think straight. Tomorrow we'll have to be really alert!"

"I guess you're right," agreed Becky, yawning. "And I'm not going to give up, ever."

"That's the spirit," Dr. Carson said. "I've still got a few surprises up my sleeve."

"Well, good night, Dad. Good night, Chip," said Becky. "Don't do anything weird tonight."

"I won't be able to," replied the android. "My fuel cell needs a full recharging after all that physical activity."

"Good night, kids," said Dr. Carson. "I'm going to do a little work here, and then I'll go to bed myself."

Early the next morning, Chip's internal alarm woke him up. His fuel cell fully recharged, he coiled the cord back into his shin and went into the living room.

Ker-slap!

The android's audio tracking program detected the faint sound of the doormat being lifted on the front porch. Racing to the window, he looked outside. "Dad!" he shouted. "I see the black van!"

Dr. Carson threw on his bathrobe as he raced

downstairs. "What are you shouting about, Chip?"

"The black van, Dad! I saw it."

Dr. Carson jumped up and peered out the window. "It's gone now, but I see another one of those letters on the front porch. Chip, did you see the numbers on the license plate?"

"No, the mud is still covering it. Do you want me to get the letter?"

"That's all right, I'll get it myself."

When Dr. Carson returned with the letter, Chip asked, "What does the letter say?"

"It's almost the same as before. He's reminding us that we've only got twelve hours left." Dr. Carson let out a heavy sigh. "Let's eat breakfast. Maybe Becky has some ideas."

A few moments later, Becky came downstairs and read the letter. "That's disgusting!" she said indignantly. "This person could ruin our lives forever! Who does this Android Master think he is, anyway?"

"That's precisely what I want to know," said her father, pouring a glass of orange juice. "Let's go over everything we have so far. But first let me see if my calculations are ready. I'll be right back." Dr. Carson ran down to the basement and returned seconds later with a long white printout.

Becky took out her notebook. "Let's get started. All we know for sure is that he, or she, drives a black van and uses this special computer printer to send us nasty letters," she said, writing it down.

"Actually, we may know a lot more than that," Dr. Carson said. "Last night, I fed all the data from the ultra-microwave direction finder into the computer downstairs, and this morning my results were ready. Using differential calculus, I was able to determine approximately where the signals started from."

"Where?" asked Becky eagerly. "That could help us a lot."

"Maybe and maybe not. Remember, if it's coming from a van, then the location may be where the van was driving when it sent the signals. And that wouldn't tell us very much."

"It might help anyway," Becky said.

"Where do the signals come from, Dad?" asked Chip.

"Harborland Shopping Center," replied the scientist. "I'm almost sure."

"Hey!" yelled Becky. "Maybe Mr. Foster's the Android Master after all. Or what about Cap? Both of their stores are at Harborland."

"I think we've pretty much eliminated both of them," said Dr. Carson. He buttered a piece of toast. "But the more I think about it, the more it seems there's one other person who's a real suspect."

"Who, Pops?"

124

"Mr. Chin, who runs the electronics store at Harborland."

"No way, Pops. He's a really nice guy."

"I know that, Becky. But we have to consider every possible suspect."

After examining his data files, Chip said, "It's logical to suspect him, Dad. He certainly has electronics and computer skills."

"And the equipment," the scientist explained softly. "Who else besides Mr. Chin knows exactly what kind of electronic parts I've been buying since I moved to Harbor City? He might have been able to figure out why I needed all the synchronized sector motors, electrologic memory circuits, and—"

"But I can't believe it," whispered Becky. "Jack Chin is a friend of ours. He was the bass player in The Deep Six."

"That, unfortunately, is another strike against Mr. Chin," Dr. Carson said grimly. "You might have accidentally let something slip in front of Jack, which he then told his father."

"But we're just guessing, right?" Becky said. She stood up to get ready for school. "We can't really be sure."

"No, but I'm going to check it out the minute school is over. I'm going to go over there and see if Mr. Chin has an Epsoki 8023 in the back room."

"Please be careful, Pops," said Becky.

125

"Come on, Chip, get that old red book bag of yours. You don't want to be late."

"He's not going to school today," said Dr. Carson.

"You can't leave him alone," Becky protested. "He might do anything! At least if he's at school, you or I can be close to him."

"I can't risk it, Becky. After what he did last night, he might do something that would endanger the lives of other students."

"Are you going to switch me off?" asked the android.

"No," Dr. Carson replied. "I need your power turned on. I'm just going to fix it so you can't leave the house. Come here, son."

Dr. Carson pulled up Chip's shirt and opened his chest hatch. He reached inside and flipped a switch.

"It always looks so strange when you open him up like that," Becky said. "What did you do?"

"He turned off all the sector motors in my legs," explained Chip. "I can't walk anywhere."

Dr. Carson gently dragged him over to a chair. "Chip, I want you awake today so you can tell me if anyone tries to give you orders. Then my direction finder will be able to trace the signal."

"I get it," said Becky. "The Android Master won't try anything if Chip is turned off, but if we leave him on like this, Chip won't be able to run away. Pops, you're a genius."

"I just hope I'm right about Mr. Chin."

"I hope you're wrong. Jack's our friend!"

"We'll know by tonight."

Becky and Dr. Carson went to school. Chip sat in the chair and waited. Nothing happened all morning except that he saw fourteen sparrows fly past the kitchen window. At noon his father called him on his internal interface radio.

"ANYTHING UNUSUAL TO REPORT?"

"NOTHING," replied the android.

"AFTER SCHOOL I'M GOING STRAIGHT TO CHIN'S, AND BECKY WILL COME HOME TO MAKE SURE YOU'RE ALL RIGHT."

"OKAY, DAD. BE CAREFUL."

"I WILL."

That afternoon the phone rang once, but Chip couldn't reach it to answer. More sparrows were sighted in the back yard. At 3:15, Becky came home.

As she was entering the house, Dr. Carson was parking the jeep in front of Chin's. He headed for the front door of the shop.

The scientist saw Mr. Chin in the display window, but before he could enter, the store owner rushed over to the front door, pulled the shade down, and hung a CLOSED sign in the window.

Dr. Carson ran to a nearby phone booth. He

dialed his home number. "Becky, I'm at Harborland. Is Chip all right?"

"I'm glad you called," Becky said. "Chip's been acting really weird. He's waving his arms around and he won't answer me."

"At least he can't go anywhere," said Dr. Carson. "Be sure to stay out of his reach."

"Don't worry. What about Mr. Chin?"

"Just as I started to go inside, he closed the store. I think he's aware that we know about him."

"What are you going to do, Pops?"

"I'm going to confront him one way or another," said Dr. Carson confidently.

"No, Pops, go get the police."

"I can't wait that long. By the time the police get here, Mr. Chin might do anything to Chip. He might even command him to tear himself apart."

"Should I turn Chip off?"

"Good idea," replied the scientist. "I'll let you know what happens."

"Please be careful, Pops," Becky pleaded. "And hurry back soon!"

Becky hung up the phone and started looking for a pencil. "Oh, good, here's one."

The android continued to wave his arms wildly, knocking over a bowl of fruit.

"Chip, I know you can't help it, but I sure wish you'd stop," she said, edging closer.

Ring! "Maybe that's Dad!" Becky grabbed

128

for the receiver. "Hello, any news?" she said urgently.

"Uh, this is Stanley Dickinson. I'm calling Dr. Carson about the ham radio flea market."

"He's not here right now." Becky dodged away from a flying saltshaker. "Can I take a message?"

"Sure. Your father wanted to know who had bought a printer from Cap Sanders at the flea market. I pay pretty close attention to make sure all of our participants pay sales tax, so I can tell you that Cap never sold a printer."

"Are you *positive?*" inquired Becky. "It's important."

"Yes, I even asked a couple of the other hams."

"Thanks, Mr. Dickinson. I'll give the message to my father."

Crash! Becky turned around and saw that Chip's chair had tipped over.

The android was on the floor.

The next thing Becky knew, he was upside down, balancing on his hands.

"Oh, no!" screamed Becky. "Chip, you're not supposed to be able to move."

The android pulled himself forward on his hands!

"You can't leave, Chip. I won't let you!" Becky tried to block his path.

Chip raced around her. He lunged at the front door, which flew open easily because the latch hadn't caught when Becky had come in earlier. Before she could grab him, he was out the door and moving down the street.

"Even on his hands he's too fast for me," Becky thought as she ran down the steps. "But I've got to try to catch up with him."

The android was completely out of sight. "Where could he have gone?" Becky wondered. "Dad'll never forgive me for not stopping him."

As Becky was sitting down on a bus stop bench to think, Dr. Carson was knocking on the door of Chin's Electronics. "Let me in!" he shouted. "I need to talk to you, Mr. Chin!"

The door opened. "We're closed now, Dr. Carson," said Mr. Chin.

"I'm in a hurry! Do you have an Epsoki 8023 printer?"

"No," Chin replied. "But I could order one for you tomorrow."

"Why not today?" demanded Dr. Carson, straining to see inside the cluttered shop.

"We're closed for inventory," explained the storekeeper. "But since you're my favorite customer, I'll help you. By the way, I have some new multiphase stepper motors in. They're very nice. I can let you have one for $29.99."

"I'll come in for a moment," said the scientist, suddenly wondering if this was all a mistake. "Say, do you have a black van?"

"This is not a car dealership," said Mr. Chin,

opening the door. "You seem upset, Dr. Carson. Come in and have some tea."

"Thank you, but I'm looking for my son, Chip. Have you seen him?"

"Not today," replied the store owner. "Too bad the rock and roll band he and Jack were in was bad for my son's grades. I'll ask Jack if he's seen Chip when he comes back from the library."

"Chip's not hiding in here somewhere?" asked Dr. Carson suspiciously.

"Of course not. But you're welcome to look around."

Feeling foolish, the scientist said, "I'm just edgy today. Chip hasn't been feeling well, and he's been acting a little strange. You haven't seen a black van around here, have you?"

"Yes, I've noticed that one's been parked in front of the store the last few weeks, but I don't know who owns it. In fact, there it is now!" Mr. Chin pointed out the display window.

Speeding around a corner of the parking lot in front of the stores was a big black van. "The rear end is covered with mud," yelled Dr. Carson, rushing out of the store.

"What about your printer?" shouted Mr. Chin. "Should I order it?"

But the scientist didn't hear him. Dr. Carson was already in his jeep and speeding after the van.

"Those Carsons are nice, but they're a little

crazy," said the storekeeper, locking his door to begin inventory.

Becky had searched everywhere but she hadn't found Chip. She walked slowly toward the waterfront. "Dad's wrong about Mr. Chin," she thought, quickening her pace. "If Cap didn't sell that printer, then he must have been lying all along! That's it! It must be Cap who's controlling Chip! I've got to get there right away." She turned around and ran as fast as she possibly could to Harborland.

When she reached the video arcade, Becky poked her head in the door. Cap wasn't there.

"Where's Cap?" she yelled to Scott over the loud music.

"I don't know, but I hope he gets back soon. I don't know how your brother did so well on this Turtle Rescue game. I can barely get past the third level."

Becky ran outside in search of Cap. She noticed that there was an apartment above the arcade, so she went around to the back to look for an entrance. There was a fire escape running up the rear of the building, but she couldn't quite reach it.

Becky dragged a large trash barrel under the ladder, scrambled onto the fire escape, and climbed up to the second floor. She looked in the window. Cap was inside. He turned around and saw Becky.

132

"What are you doing out there?" demanded Cap, rushing to the window. "Spying on me?"

"I'm looking for my brother, Chip," said Becky. "I wasn't spying."

"I don't believe you," said the arcade owner. "What would your brother be doing up here?"

Becky tried to see past Cap, but he filled most of the window. "You haven't seen him downstairs?"

"Not today," Cap replied. "Why don't you come inside and take the front stairs down? You could fall off that rickety old fire escape."

He made a grab for Becky's hand and missed.

All of a sudden, she caught a glimpse of something on the floor of the apartment. It was Chip's wallet!

"What have you done to my brother?" yelled Becky. "That's his wallet!"

"How would his wallet get inside my apartment?" asked the arcade owner, making another grab for Becky's hand.

"If he was walking on his hands he might lose it," she shouted, edging back.

Cap reached out the window as far as he could. Finally grabbing Becky's hand, he pulled her inside the apartment.

Becky fell onto the floor and snatched the wallet. "It's my brother's all right," she said angrily. "Touch me again and I'll bite your hand off."

"You might at that," said Cap. He reached behind him and pulled a rope out of a drawer. "You should've stayed home, Miss Carson. Now I'll have to figure out some way to get rid of you."

"Come any closer and you'll be sorry. I'll scream my head off!"

"Ha," laughed Cap. "No one can hear you over the noise downstairs."

"Where's my brother?" demanded Becky.

"He's in the next room."

She made a daring break for the door. Cap was after her in a flash. She darted away and plunged into the next room. Chip was tied to a chair with steel cables.

"I'll get the police, Chip, don't worry," yelled Becky, racing for the front door.

"It's locked, Becky," said Chip. "It only opens with a key."

Becky grabbed at the door and pulled with all her strength, but the android was right. "Why are you doing this, Cap?" she yelled. "We've never done anything to you."

"That's what you think," replied Cap, inching forward, the rope coiled and ready. "Your father made me suffer in a hundred different ways. I've been planning my revenge for years. I'll convince the world that this C-13 Integrated Electrologic Android is my invention and I'll get all the credit, maybe even the Nobel prize. I want to destroy your father's career because he destroyed mine."

"I don't know what you're talking about. You didn't invent Chip," protested Becky. "Dad did! What am I saying? Nobody invented Chip, he's just a boy."

"You don't have to pretend, Becky," Cap said arrogantly. "I've known about Chip almost as long as you've been alive. He is *my* creation! I've been controlling him these last few days, and I even ordered him to act as a microphone and transmitter so I could hear everything inside your house."

"Listen," snapped Becky. "If you let us go, we won't tell anybody."

"Not a chance, young lady."

"My father knows I was coming here, and somebody must have seen Chip come in."

"Nobody saw me," the android replied. "I was ordered to come to the back entrance when nobody was looking. Cap lowered the fire escape and I climbed up with my hands."

"Listen, little Missy Carson. I'm not worried about your father one bit. He's out chasing a black van," said Cap with a laugh. "It's remote-controlled and programmed to go over the cliff north of town on Route 58. If your father's following closely enough, he won't be able to stop in time."

Becky charged at Cap. "Give me that key!"

she yelled, trying to reach into his pockets. But he was much stronger and easily wrapped the rope around her. Moments later, Becky was tied to a chair beside her brother.

"My dad will find us," threatened Becky. "You can't get away with this."

"I'm *really* worried," Cap said sarcastically. "Besides, I've already gotten away with it. As soon as I close up the arcade, I'm leaving this town for good."

"I'll scream."

"Go ahead! I already told you, no one can hear you. I've gotten quite sick of this arcade, though it *was* a good cover. Even your father looked me right in the eye and didn't recognize me."

"You mean your beard, the eye patch, and the hat are all a disguise?" Becky asked, examining him carefully.

"The hat's real," said Cap, laughing at his own joke. "But the rest of it is as phony as the great Dr. Jonas Carson."

"Dad's not a phony," Chip said.

"You're programmed to say that," replied Cap. "But when I get through with you, you'll tell the world who the greatest android designer is."

"You must be crazy," Becky exclaimed. "Who cares who's the greatest android designer? Dad's never said he was the greatest."

"And he's not," Cap answered. "I am. You

two will have to wait here a few minutes, because I'm going downstairs to close up the arcade. Then we're going for a long trip. Or at least Chip and I are. I don't know what I'll do with you."

"You let me go right now," demanded Becky, pounding her feet on the floor.

"It's your own fault," said Cap, unlocking the door. "You should have stayed home like a nice girl."

"You're going to find out that I'm not so nice," Becky screamed, as he slammed the door behind him. Turning to Chip, she asked, "Do you know who that psycho is?"

"His name is Cap," replied Chip.

"Yeah, but that's just a nickname."

"Since the printer was registered to George Sanders," said the android, "it would be logical that Sanders is his real name."

"I don't think so. He seems to know Dad, but Dad didn't recognize that name." Becky struggled with the rope. "We've got to get out of here. Call Dad on your internal interface radio."

"I can't," replied Chip. "It's being jammed."

"Can you move over and see out the back window?"

"Yes," Chip replied, shifting from side to side until he reached the window.

"Do you see anybody? Maybe you could yell."

Scanning the parking lot behind the arcade, the android said, "I see Erin."

"This is one time when I want her to see you," ordered Becky. "Yell as loudly as you can."

"HHEEYY, ERRRINNNN!"

Becky flinched in pain. "Did she hear you?"

"She didn't turn her head," reported Chip. "Should I yell again?"

"I don't think it will do any good. Erin didn't hear you the first time. Is there some way to make your voice louder? Wait!" she cried. "You remember how you got the stove to talk the other day? Can you do that again?"

"No," answered the android. "Dad told me not to."

"Chip!" Becky yelled in frustration. "Do it now. Dad would want you to do it in order to save our lives."

"All right," he said. "I'm programmed to protect all humans. I see a car out the window and I can vibrate its hood magnetically to produce synthetic vocal sounds."

"Great," said Becky. "Go ahead."

"Hey, Erin, I need your help!" Erin jumped back when she heard the mechanical voice.

"Who are you?" she asked, frantically looking around. The sound seemed to be coming from a red station wagon. She inched closer to investigate.

Chip turned his audio tracking program to high volume so he could hear Erin's replies.

"It's me, Chip Carson."

"No it's not, don't try to fool me."

"Yes, Erin, it's really me."

"I don't know who you are, but I'm not going to stick around so you can make fun of me. Goodbye!"

"Wait!" yelled Chip. "Believe me, Erin. I need your help."

"How can I believe you?"

"Because I know who your favorite person is."

"Everyone knows *that!*" Erin said sarcastically.

"Will you believe that I really am Chip Carson if I tell you that I know you are planning a surprise party for your dad this weekend?"

"How did you know that? The only person who knows is . . . CHIP! Is it really you? How can you make your voice do that? Where are you hiding?"

"I'm upstairs in the apartment over Cap's Arcade. Get the police."

"What?" cried Erin. "You aren't playing a trick on me, are you?"

"No," replied Chip. "Becky and I are in big trouble. Cap has kidnapped us. We really need your help."

Erin studied the rear of the building. All of a

sudden she spotted Chip's head through the second-story window. "I see you, I see you!" she exclaimed.

"Tell the police to rescue us and to stop my dad. He's in danger," said the android. "He's following a remote-controlled black van that's driving north on Route 58."

"I'll do it right now," she yelled, racing to the nearest phone booth.

"What's Erin doing?" Becky asked, struggling with her ropes.

"She's dialing the police," answered Chip.

"I take back everything I ever said about her," said Becky. "She may have a one-track mind, but she sure comes through when you need her."

"I see a lot of kids moving out into the parking lot," reported the android. "Cap must have closed the arcade."

"That's right," said Cap, coming back into the room. "I don't have to pretend anymore. As soon as it gets dark, we'll leave this boring town. And don't you dare make any noise now, girlie," he said to Becky. "One sound out of you and you'll be sorry."

"Where are we going?" asked Chip. "Can my dad come, too?"

"He's probably driving over a cliff right now," laughed Cap. He began packing electronic equipment into boxes. "You two just sit

140

tight while I get ready. Ha, ha, as if you had any other choice.''

Chip looked out into the parking lot. After a few minutes, he saw two police cars pull up. They didn't have their sirens on. "Don't worry, Becky, things will be all right," he said.

"Shut up," ordered Cap. "I should turn you off, but I want to make sure I don't do it wrong."

"If I tell you how to turn him off, will you let me go free?" asked Becky. "You could drop me off at the edge of town when you leave."

"Maybe," replied Cap. "Tell me how."

"Stick a pencil in his right ear. That's his master reset switch. I've done it plenty of times."

Cap moved toward Chip and pushed a pencil into his ear.

Eeeeeeeeee! "What's that noise?" he yelled, pulling the pencil back. "You're trying to trick me."

Suddenly the door splintered open. "Put your hands up!" yelled a police officer, gun drawn.

"I can't," said Chip. "My hands are tied."

"Not you," said the officer, rushing into the room. "Hands up, Cap. Don't cause me any trouble."

Three more police officers burst in behind him. Chip recognized two of them. "Hi, Officer Bailey. Hi, Officer Simpson."

"Be quiet, Chip!" commanded Becky.

With his hands in the air, Cap was edging toward a large box with an antenna on top.

"Don't even think of touching anything, Cap," declared the officer, pointing the gun straight at him.

"Why not?" Before the officer could stop him, Cap slammed his hand down on a button on top of the box.

Blam! A bullet whizzed over Cap's head. "Touch anything else and I'll do more than fire a warning shot," the officer said, keeping his gun aimed at Cap.

"I'll go peacefully," replied Cap. "I've gotten my revenge."

"What did you do?" Becky cried, as Officer Simpson untied her. "Did you blow up that van or something?"

"Something is right!" Cap said. "Remember that stereo your android won? That was really a bomb. I blew up your house!"

"Oh no!" cried Becky. "You didn't! Not our house!"

"Don't worry," said Dr. Carson as he came into the room. "Luckily for all of us, when the state police pulled me over and told me that Cap had kidnapped you, I suspected that the stereo he gave you might be a bomb. The police sent a bomb squad to our house and defused it in time." Striding over to Cap, he asked angrily,

"Okay, mister, why did you kidnap my children and try to blow up my house?"

"You really don't recognize me, do you?" said Cap defiantly. He pulled off his beard, blue hat, and eye patch. Instead of an old sea captain, he was a young man in his twenties. Hatred burned in his eyes.

"Gordon, Gordon Vogel?" the scientist said with surprise. "My lab assistant from college? I never would have guessed you were smart enough to pull this off."

"You stole my research!" shouted Vogel. "I can prove it."

"My dad would never steal anything," Chip said. "He's told me that stealing is wrong."

"I didn't steal anybody's research, Gordon," said Dr. Carson, trying to hold his temper. "When you worked for me you were always giving me harebrained suggestions that wouldn't work in a million years. I never even thought of using any of your so-called ideas. They were sloppy and unscientific. You thought you were a great genius, but you never raised a finger to prove it. When you kept making mistakes, I had to fire you. But that's no reason to kidnap my children."

"After you fired me, I wasn't able to get another research job," said Vogel angrily. "I had to become a stupid video game repairman to earn a living."

143

"Come on, Cap," said Officer Bailey, putting the handcuffs on him. "You'll have plenty of time to tell all this to a judge. They'll go pretty rough on you. Kidnapping is a serious crime."

"Stop," said Vogel, struggling to break free. "I didn't kidnap anyone. Becky came up on my fire escape on her own. And Chip isn't a kid, he's just an android!"

Thinking quickly, Becky shouted, "Don't call my brother dirty names!"

"Yeah," said Officer Simpson. "Watch your language around these kids, Cap!"

"Let's take him down to the station," Officer Bailey said, tugging Vogel by his handcuffs. "Dr. Carson, we'll want you and your children to make a statement. But the evidence here is pretty obvious."

"I just can't understand it," replied the scientist. "He must have hated me for all these years."

"I still do," snarled Vogel, as they took him downstairs. "Chip Carson's an android, I tell you. A robot! Just look at him!"

As soon as everyone was gone, Dr. Carson quickly reached under Chip's shirt and activated his leg motors. Then the three of them walked downstairs. Erin was waiting there for them.

"Chip, are you all right?" she cried, rushing into his arms.

"I'm fine," replied the android.

"Erin, we owe you a lot," said Becky. "If you hadn't heard Chip yelling at you, we might still be up there."

"I don't understand it," said Erin, letting the android go. "How could Chip make his voice do that? And why was that guy calling him a robot?"

"I'm not a robot," Chip answered, "I'm—"

"A ventriloquist," Becky interrupted. "Cap sure turned out to be a genuine lunatic, let me tell you. He was babbling all kinds of nonsense about Chip."

"Let's go home, kids," said Dr. Carson. "I've had enough adventure for one day. I'm almost in a state of shock. I can't understand why Gordon Vogel would do all those terrible things."

"He was jealous, Pops," Becky said. "And obviously a loser. Imagine, going around every day wearing a false beard and a fake eye patch."

"He fooled all of us," said Erin. "What a sicko."

Dr. Carson turned to her and placed his hand on her shoulder. "Erin, we are very grateful for what you've done."

"Yeah, Erin," agreed Becky reluctantly. "Thanks a lot. I'm sorry I was—"

"Oh, that's okay. I did it for Chip," she said. "Maybe now you won't mind if I interview him."

"You can interview him tomorrow," said Dr.

Carson. "But tonight we just want to go straight home."

"I can understand that," Erin replied. "Did the doctors find out what's wrong with Chip?"

"Oh yes, and he's *completely* cured now," said Becky.

"And I'm completely starved and exhausted," Dr. Carson added. "Let's go!"

"See you tomorrow," said Erin, waving goodbye.

When the Carson family pulled up in front of their house, Jake Blocker was sitting on the front steps waiting for them.

"Hi, Chip," said Jake. "Ready to help me with my homework? Hey, why is everybody groaning?"

Activity books

Beginners Series
Eric Dominy
Judo for Beginners £1.25 ☐

Robert Fenton
Chess for Beginners £1.25 ☐

Drawings is Easy Series
Felix Lorenzi
Animals £1.95 ☐
People £1.95 ☐
Perspective £1.95 ☐
Nature £1.95 ☐

Dwight and Patricia Harris
Computer Programming 1, 2, 3! £1.25 ☐

Margaret Crush
Handy Homes for Creepy Crawlies 95p ☐
Trace Your Family Tree £1.50 ☐
Town Trail £1.50 ☐

Nature Notebooks
Mammals £1.50 ☐
Insects £1.50 ☐
Birds £1.50 ☐
Wild Flowers £1.50 ☐

David Scott
Children's All-Star Cook Book £1.25 ☐

Mary Peplow and Debra Shipley
London Fun Book £1.50 ☐

To order direct from the publisher just tick the titles you want
and fill in the order form. D7A

Fiction in paperback from Dragon Books

Peter Glidewell

Schoolgirl Chums	£1.25	☐
St Ursula's in Danger	£1.25	☐
Miss Prosser's Passion	£1.50	☐

Enid Gibson

The Lady at 99	£1.50	☐

Gerald Frow

Young Sherlock: The Mystery of the Manor House	95p	☐
Young Sherlock: The Adventure at Ferryman's Creek	£1.50	☐

Frank Richards

Billy Bunter of Greyfriars School	£1.25	☐
Billy Bunter's Double	£1.25	☐
Billy Bunter Comes for Christmas	£1.25	☐
Billy Bunter Does His Best	£1.25	☐
Billy Bunter's Benefit	£1.50	☐
Billy Bunter's Postal Order	£1.50	☐

Dale Carlson
Jenny Dean Mysteries

Mystery of the Shining Children	£1.50	☐
Mystery of the Hidden Trap	£1.50	☐
Secret of the Third Eye	£1.50	☐

Marlene Fanta Shyer

My Brother the Thief	95p	☐

David Rees

The Exeter Blitz	£1.50	☐

Caroline Akrill

Eventer's Dream	£1.50	☐
A Hoof in the Door	£1.50	☐
Ticket to Ride	£1.50	☐

Michel Parry (ed)

Superheroes	£1.25	☐

Ulick O'Connor

Irish Tales and Sagas	£2.95	☐

To order direct from the publisher just tick the titles you want
and fill in the order form.

Activity and non-fiction books
Micro Adventures

Space Attack	£1.50	☐
Jungle Quest	£1.50	☐
Million Dollar Gamble	£1.50	☐
Time Trap	£1.50	☐
Mindbenders	£1.50	☐
Robot Race	£1.50	☐

Golden Dragon Fantasy Gamebooks
Dave Morris

Crypt of the Vampire	£1.50	☐
The Eye of the Dragon	£1.50	☐
Castle of Lost Souls	£1.50	☐

Oliver Johnson

The Lord of Shadow Keep	£1.50	☐
Curse of the Pharaoh	£1.50	☐

Dave Morris and Oliver Johnson

The Temple of Flame	£1.50	☐

History
Everyday Lives

Prehistoric Times	£1.95	☐
Ancient Egypt	£1.95	☐
Roman Times	£1.95	☐
Knights and Castles	£1.95	☐
The Age of Discovery	£1.95	☐
The Wild West	£1.95	☐

W V Butler

Young Detective's Whodunnit	£1.25	☐
Foiled Again	£1.50	☐

Brian Ball

Young Person's Guide to UFO's	95p	☐

Bernard Brett·

Young Person's Guide to Ghosts	85p	☐

To order direct from the publisher just tick the titles you want
and fill in the order form.

All these books are available at your local bookshop or newsagent, or can be ordered direct from the publisher.

To order direct from the publishers just tick the titles you want and fill in the form below.

Name _____

Address _____

_____

Send to:
Dragon Cash Sales
PO Box 11, Falmouth, Cornwall TR10 9EN.

Please enclose remittance to the value of the cover price plus:

UK 45p for the first book, 20p for the second book plus 14p per copy for each additional book ordered to a maximum charge of £1.63.

BFPO and Eire 45p for the first book, 20p for the second book plus 14p per copy for the next 7 books, thereafter 8p per book.

Overseas 75p for the first book and 21p for each additional book.

Dragon Books reserve the right to show new retail prices on covers, which may differ from those previously advertised in the text or elsewhere.